Outlaw from the Concordat

A shape amid the shadows, the assassin stalked the sentry. As the youthful soldier came to the end of his round, he breathed out, glanced around, and turned on his heel to return. Something stood before him, its face inches from him. For long moments nothing happened, with the sentry frozen in near-shock, and Tyler standing motionless at the boy's front, eyeing him. The sentry twitched, obviously beginning to think about shouting or fleeing. Tyler reached up, and, without effort, pulled off his victim's helmet.

"What . . . ?" the soldier began, and filled his lungs to shout. Tyler's knotted fist impacted savagely upon the inexperienced sentry's temple. He caught the sagging form before the combat rifle could clatter to the ground . . .

Other Avon Books by
Jefferson P. Swycaffer

BECOME THE HUNTED
NOT IN OUR STARS

Coming Soon

THE PRAESIDIUM OF ARCHIVE

THE UNIVERSAL PREY

JEFFERSON P. SWYCAFFER

AVON
PUBLISHERS OF BARD, CAMELOT, DISCUS AND FLARE BOOKS

Several of the concepts and nomenclatures used in this story are from the games Imperium™ and Traveller®, published by Game Designers' Workshop and designed by Marc W. Miller, to whom I give all my thanks for his kind permission regarding this use.

Some of the background situations depicted in this novel appeared in an article entitled "Exonidas Spaceport" published in issue No. 59 (March 1982) of Dragon® Magazine, edited by Kim Mohan, to whom I am also very grateful and professionally indebted.

J.P.S.

THE UNIVERSAL PREY is an original publication of Avon Books. This work has never before appeared in book form. This work is a novel. Any similarity to actual persons or events is purely coincidental.

AVON BOOKS
A division of
The Hearst Corporation
1790 Broadway
New York, New York 10019

Copyright © 1985 by Jefferson P. Swycaffer
Published by arrangement with the author
Library of Congress Catalog Card Number: 85-90654
ISBN: 0-380-89662-1

First Avon Printing, October 1985

AVON TRADEMARK REG. U.S. PAT. OFF. AND IN OTHER COUNTRIES, MARCA REGISTRADA, HECHO EN U.S.A.

Printed in the U.S.A.

WFH   10   9   8   7   6   5   4   3   2   1

This book is dedicated to Rod O'Riley and to David Proctor, and all the other hackers at SkR-APA who delight in wordplay, both serious and frivolous.

When dreams themselves do dream,
And the gaze of spiders is upon us,
Your laughter strikes away the dark.
I grasp your hand tightly.

Anon.

The computer file lay in a neat bundle on the cluttered desk of Admiral Higgins of Concordat Naval Intelligence. Printed on the palest mint-green paper, bound in a dark-green clip, it was propped open to its title page, and a heavy antique brass ruler lay across it to keep the place. Although the lights in the plush room were extinguished, the slowly blinking green light of the desktop computer terminal illuminated the manuscript indistinctly, and reflected highlights from the shiny metal of the ruler.

James Tyler, the opening page read, in a smooth and precise machine typeface. *Commander, Concordat Navy*.

James Tyler stood on the lip of a precipice high in the mountains of the world on which he'd been stationed for no more than three months. An icy wind blew in gusts from behind him, whipping past his head and out into the gulf. Patchy, coiling fog closed the sphere of visibility down to a scant few meters; the cliff face below him could be seen dropping away into rubble that seemed to fall forever.

Even in his foam-filled jacket he felt the biting chill, but chose to ignore it. Beneath his wind-tossed blond hair, cold gray eyes strove to pierce the limitless mist. His tall, slim frame rocked slightly to the booming gusts. His hands were in his jacket pockets, tightly clenched. His mind held the blackness of unending night.

Assassin, read the printout. *Twenty kills. Four failures. Wounded six times. Loyalty extremely questionable. His contact is through the Black Book.*

*   *   *

Beneath Tyler's left arm hung a well-worn automatic pistol, his favorite. He'd killed both men and women with other weapons, some of them sick and sickening, but he'd always preferred this pistol.

The air moaned; the streamers of fog whipped past him, merging with the encircling mist that hung like a curtain, closing off the view. And the frigid voice of the wind asked repetitiously, whispering, shouting, indistinct: *What now?*

As from all intimate confrontations, James Tyler turned away and bent to the chill blast, walking the few meters to his ground car. He saw no escape from the life that he despised. He unlatched the driver's-side door, which the wind yanked from his hand. Easing into the warm interior, he pulled the door shut against the mocking wind.

Without expression he pushed his hair back from his eyes and turned the car toward the distant city.

One hundred and twelve standard days earlier.

The swollen sun of late spring shone painfully down onto the greens and grays of the seaport city of Exonidas. Native birds squabbled with off-planet species for roosting spots, neither of the two populations quite knowing what to make of the other. A steady stream of people walked stiffly or sauntered easily along the crowded sidewalks of the city's vice district. In the district's heart, traffic was thick, moving coolly past the doors of Lady Titania's, a brothel nestled comfortably between two nondescript storefronts.

Drug sniffers slouched by, oblivious to anything but the sensuous pounding that swelled their balloon-empty heads. Opportunists stalked by, eyes alert for chance encounters they could turn to their advantage. Officers of the state walked unobtrusively, only narrowly failing to merge into the flow of vice that they strove to guide, not to stem. Staid businessmen, here either for furtive pleasure or simply on their way somewhere else—anywhere else—strode stiffly, their locked briefcases clutched in their cold hands.

And among this collection were the few that were solitary and threatening. There were the crazies, the straights, the cold-sellers, the fearful and those on the run; there were the swift, the silent, the deadly.

The morning droned on toward noon. Among the masses of moving people wove a tall figure in tight, informal clothing. Ignoring the crowds and by them ignored he made his way closer to the doorway to Lady Titania's. He entered without slackening his pace; and yet his watchful tension suggested that whatever he found within would not surprise him.

The headmistress greeted him coolly. Without seeming to notice her, the man tossed down a thick bundle of cash and demanded, "The key to seventeen, please."

The headmistress slid the cash into a collection slot and flipped the key onto the desk. The man scooped it up and walked away. She watched him, her eyes narrowing in uneasy curiosity. It might be her house, but she had no inkling of what might be found behind cubicle seventeen's locked door. All of the other cubicles—unlocked—had beds, showers, and waiting, willing girls. Number seventeen had only mystery. The headmistress, however, was very certain there was no girl in that cubicle. She had her own ideas about what waited for this cold-looking customer but suspected all of them were wrong. With an idle glance down the corridor, she returned to her well-thumbed magazine.

Down the soft-carpeted hallway the man walked, ignoring the several closed and inviting doors to either side. Partway along, three doors stood open. Lounging near them were the three young women who were assigned these cubicles; they stood casually by, exchanging news and gossip, pretending not to see the man.

Glory, all blonde curls and great blue eyes, sniffed audibly as the man passed her; Sylvia and Jill were silent. They were curious enough to make a guessing game of what awaited the very few customers who were allowed inside cubicle seventeen. Sylvia allowed herself an honest jealousy, for she found the stranger's trim build quite attractive. Jill, probably the most perceptive of the three, thought she sensed a vulnerability to the man, in the way his face was averted—almost—as he passed.

Seemingly unaware of the three young women, the man made his way to cubicle seventeen. He unlocked the door, at the same time pressing the small, all-but-invisible catch near the doorknob. The door swung open, letting the man into the darkened room.

With the door shut, and the light snapped on, he stepped forward to the bare table that sat in the center of the otherwise empty chamber. This, then, was the Black Book: a misnomer, for no book *per se* was involved. Placing his hand on the center of the table, he said aloud, "James Tyler." And because he knew that someday his words would be heard by someone tending the machinery, he added, "What've you got, fellow?'"

Through the top of the table a sheet of paper materialized, melting upward as if revealed by a fading mist. When it was fully solid, Tyler snatched it up.

"P. Empellimin, this world, Theury Continent, nation of Vistheur, wilderness north of Vis city, immediate."

Immediate, eh? Tyler thought sardonically. *Give me ten days, and Empellimin is cats' meat.* In his hand the fateful sheet of paper foamed, writhed, melted away.

For Tyler, the next part was the hardest: waiting for just over an hour in the harshly lit room with nothing to occupy his mind. Form demanded that he give the curious witnesses enough time to imagine whatever they might wish, following illusory hints to misleading and false conclusions.

Theury continent, Tyler thought wryly. It was a rough assignment. Theury continent was a wasteland, devastated by an all-too-recent nuclear war that had been limited to that half of the planet. Seen from orbit, the continent was a long, north-south oriented ellipse, wrinkled with lengthwise mountain ranges, the highest on the planet. Vast deserts, great harbors, and millions of square kilometers of forests had made the continent potentially the richest area anywhere in the world.

Instead, political division had forced the diversion of much of the region's wealth into the buildup of armies, navies, air and close-orbit forces, and a nuclear deterrent force, one of each for each of the five major nations that divided the continent. When two of the nations, disgusted at the waste, had united, the remaining three did likewise; within a week all five were dead. Almost eight billion people had died in that day-long war; hundreds of millions more had died from privation during the five weeks since.

Horla continent, wherein lay Exonidas city and a brothel containing James Tyler, had been spared due to its distance, its strict protestations of neutrality, and the fact that none of the five Theury nations cared to drop missiles on the Horlans while live Theurans waited to be fried.

By the time that the greater interstellar body, the Concordat, had fully understood the danger, one of its planets was more than half dead. Nothing could be done; but due to the imperatives of government, something must be attempted. On Theury continent, a vast rebuilding and rescue effort was being raised from the hastily constructed Emergency Spaceport at the southern tip of the continent. The spaceport city, with its full population of ten thousand, was built on the site of a Theuran city that had once boasted ten million citizens.

So, thought Tyler, *if people want to ruin their own planets, why not? What business is it of the gray old men that run the Concordat?*

In the meantime, several hundred thousand survivors struggled to live on the wrecked corpse of a continent that had once harbored just over eight billion. Barter and banditry were the rule in the remnants of five nations that had sent men to the stars.

Well, if I'm to kill 'P. Empellimin,' I'll need to know who he is . . . or was. Bandit chief, or leader of a revival faction? Hiding in the mountains or in the forests? Was he even still alive?

The time was up, and the door was now unlocked. Tyler rose from the floor where he had been sitting, stretched, and headed for the exit, relieved to be free after the dull hour of inactivity.

Outside, in the hallway, the three girls, standing about in curiosity, jumped back, startled, as Tyler emerged. He, for the briefest instant, was also surprised. He had expected to step out into an empty hall, but found himself surrounded by three very beautiful women, each clad in tight, daring attire that was coyly demure while being riveting. The girls themselves were moving back from him, while trying to peer around him at the room from which he'd come. Still off-balance from his surprise, he carried himself forward among them. For what reason he couldn't have said—an admixture of tension released and of startlement returned—he reached out and pinched Glory's ear, swatted Sylvia playfully on the behind, and pulled Jill to him for a long intimate kiss. She didn't struggle, not wishing to fight for her dignity, and knowing that nothing worse was forthcoming. Instead she playfully returned the kiss.

Tyler released her, and stood back, a little bit embarrassed at his own forwardness. Jill regarded him coolly.

"No time to stay longer," he said at last. "I've got to run." Something in him urged him to say more; the gaze they had exchanged was—for the instant it lasted—inquisitive, alert, alive. Feeling slightly confused, as if he had come out on the wrong end of the prank, Tyler broke away and hurried for the door, tossing the key to cubicle seventeen onto the desk of the bored headmistress, who had seen none of the exchange.

"Are you going to let him get away with that?" Glory asked Jill viciously, rubbing her ear where Tyler had tweaked it.

Jill gazed down the empty hallway in the direction that Tyler had fled. Thoughtfully, a faraway look on her averted face, she answered, "Yeah."

*   *   *

James Tyler arrived at Emergency city early the next day, disembarking from the twice-daily flight from the rescue and reconstruction central base on Horla continent. Emergency Airport, with the fuel tanks of its spaceport towering in the background, was, like all the city, a quickly-thrown-together prefabricated installation. Gray ash blew in gritty gusts across the landing grids, and the skies were perpetually turbulent and dark. The city appeared out of place, as if it had recently materialized upon the site of the old city—now reduced to rows of flattened buildings. These had all toppled in the same direction, out toward the new base, away from the burst of several bombs farther inland toward the city's center. The appearance of endless rows of dead structures marching over each other, kneeling to the new seacoast base, was alarming; if stared at for too long, they seemed to move, advancing and falling, endlessly.

The skyline was bare; the canyons were mud-clogged streams without greenery to hold back the sliding soil; the area of ground zero was a blackened, cracked zone, devoid of feature or relief.

Even Tyler's cynical mind was moved to a sick, saddened realization of the waste, the senseless and horrible waste that had shattered all the cities of this continent.

In Emergency city rescue central he found a willing and informative files clerk, who, with a little proper urging, opened his data files for Tyler's quick covert inspection. He found five groups recorded here: people known to be alive; people known to be dead; names of people that the survivors had once known, alive or dead; and the great file of the unknown, filed as often as not by *ad hoc* identity number rather than by name. Old census records, phone directories, subscription lists, and whatever else of that nature had survived were coded into the computers. Each name had a suffix: L for the living, # for the dead, and the great majority of ? for unknown.

Under "Empellimin, P.," Tyler found the following entry.

Potok Ordon Empellimin. Second Military Security Prefect of the nation of Vistheur. Fourth in command of the Secretariat of the Ter-Vis alliance, the formation of which triggered the war. He was believed to have ordered the first missiles to be launched against the Ta-Sa-Is alliance, and may thus be considered the direct murderer of nearly eight billion individuals.

A photo was attached, which Tyler had duplicated. After a moment's hesitation, he punched into the remote keyboard the instruction that would change the ? notation on Empellimin's file to an emphatic #.

Passing the clerk, who had watched, silent and seemingly uninterested, Tyler slipped him a small packet of bills, rewarding the gentleman for his complicity. The clerk nodded, as if distracted, and did not appear to observe the assassin leaving.

Commander Charles Denis of the recovery and rescue force met Tyler in the waiting room of the office he shared with five other Emergency city officials, invited him in, and found chairs. It was Denis's city, for the time being, and he ran it well, with an administrator's eye and an artist's hand.

"Commander, Concordat Navy?" Denis asked, glancing again over Tyler's identification. It looked authentic, but Denis knew well enough that he was incapable of spotting a really good forgery. Denis was willing to accept Tyler's word on the matter.

"What can I do for you?"

"I'm here to investigate this planet's status with respect to its continued independence. There's been a lot of talk upstairs about annexing it outright, and more about installing a planetary governor with full powers of decree."

Denis frowned. "I'm against that, of course."

Tyler interrupted what Denis was about to say next. "Why?"

"I'm not a local; I came here with the rescue mission. The Concordat Ambassador died with this city. But his job, more than anything else, was to guarantee this world's freedom."

"Freedom to kill themselves?"

"They had every chance to work this out to a sensible solution." Denis fought to keep his voice even. He didn't have complete faith in this line of reasoning, but he intended to fight for it. "This catastrophe wasn't necessary. It was fully avoidable."

Tyler smiled sardonically.

"Dammit, Commander, it was!" Denis snapped. "The hell that was unleashed here was the result of an extremely unlikely series of blunders on the part of everyone concerned." He took a deep breath. "The Ter-Vis alliance—the countries of Tertheur and Vistheur—forced the issue and the war . . . but not deliberately. We don't know exactly why they fired at the last minute. Maybe they thought they could win."

Denis shrugged, and stared for a moment at something on his desktop. "Well, it's over. Perhaps Concordat ownership—yes, ownership!—could have prevented it. Perhaps. For myself, I feel that it could have.

"But further intervention can only confuse the long and difficult recovery that lies ahead."

Tyler heard him out without comment. Personally, he didn't care in the least what happened to this world, or who its masters were to be. However, it was his cover, arranged for him where the greater decisions were made, to be interested in the matter. It further occurred to him that even if his cover didn't compel him to debate with this Denis, he would anyway. The man's sense of righteousness incensed Tyler, who himself knew no moral code, and believed in no right or wrong beyond what served his own ends. That Denis actually believed in the correctness of what he said only further outraged the assassin, and it was with chill satisfaction that he took up the gauntlet.

"They only killed seven-and-three-quarters billion people, after all," Tyler said quietly. "Some survivors were left—to prepare for next time!" His gray eyes blazed as he hurled the last words into Denis's face. All eyes in the room swung briefly toward the two, then swung guiltily away.

"I . . ." Denis began.

"Horla continent has—what, fifteen nations?—all of which will be in the race to colonize the rich and teeming wilderness that the Theurans have just opened up. There's real estate for the taking . . . and, of course, the Horlans will behave correctly and properly toward the surviving Theurans, and toward each other." The sarcasm dripped from his voice; Denis's face turned paler.

"Surely there'll be no military advantage sought by the expanding nations; no strategic concern given to what areas are grabbed. They'll cooperate fully, dividing the spoils as gentlemen always do.

"How many nuclear missiles do the Horlan nations have stockpiled? Only a few . . . a few thousand. 'But they're *small* ones,' you object."

Tyler's voice grew more reasonable. "The people of this planet are of Concordat origin. Finding this planet without intelligent native life, they applied for, and received, permission to colonize. Then they went further. Having proven themselves self-sufficient, they applied for the unprecedented right to be an independent planet. The Praesidium, for some unknown reason, granted this status. An Ambassador was sent to aid them and to help coordinate their trade with the Concordat, to the profit of both. The Concordat is not so proud an empire—empire, dammit!—that they couldn't afford to allow one small hole in the continuity of their suzerainty.

"Due to this oversight, billions have died. Planetary independence was to the profit of the premiers, presidents, kings, and governors of this world's nations. It was to the profit of the world's manufacturers, shippers, importers, exporters, bankers, brokers, and owners. How many such are now alive? How well is their precious freedom of economy faring?

"Was it worth it?"

Denis sat motionless, not able to answer. Tyler sat forward on his chair, his body in a bitter attitude, the blood darkening his face. And this was from one who did not believe in his argument, but was only looking for a fight.

Denis shook himself. "Freedom," he said in a thin voice, "is always worth it. A man in chains is no more alive than is a man burned away."

He might have said more, but Tyler's wrath shriveled him in his seat.

" 'Better death than slavery,' eh, old friend? 'See, while I hold the gun to my son's head *and to yours*, that I would rather all of us die than pay your seven percent taxes.' If that's the tune you're singing, I say to hell with you." He stood. "I'll need a helicopter and a transport permit. If you're so all-fired fond of your damnable freedom, then you'll have both waiting for me when I get to the airport."

He stalked from the room, snatching his cap from the table where he'd dropped it, and, in a totally unnecessary gesture, kicking the door loose from its hinges as he left. Let the world beware, his rage sang, Tyler's on the loose. The men and women in the office glanced from the pallid and shaken Denis to the door, tilted in its frame. One of the secretaries, without waiting for formal permission, hurriedly phoned in the requisition for a copter and a travel permit.

Tyler arrived at the airport feeling sick. Headsick, heartsick, gutsick. His eyes and head ached, his mouth tasted foul to him, and his stomach churned. Like a man recovering from a drug or liquor jag, he stomped through the airport, asking directions occasionally in a hushed yet dangerous tone. At last he found his helicopter, and with it his travel permit. He'd known that they would be waiting for him. Denis would never dare to again confront the man who had so devastated him.

Tyler wanted to vomit from the strain of that performance. Swallowing again and again, he signalled for the tram that would bring his luggage from where he'd left it. When it arrived, he threw the three small cases onto the helicopter and dragged himself in after.

Airports, as a rule, object to unscheduled takeoffs and landings; Tyler, as a rule, objected to rules, and violated them whenever it was convenient. Glancing about the cramped cockpit, he nodded, threw the ignition over, and without further ado hurled the machine straight up and into the sky. No roar of outrage came from the radio, for he had carefully neglected to switch it on.

At a comfortable cruising altitude, he fled northward at full speed. From the air the devastation was worse than he'd imagined possible. Thousands of square kilometers of low hills, valleys, and broad mesas were blackened, ruined, fire-scarred with the important difference that the fire had been thermonuclear. If an ordinary fire had swept through this area—an impossibility under sane circumstances—by this time, some five weeks after the disaster, a fine green grassy growth would have been visible, as buried grass seeds put up their tender shoots, luxuriating in the fire-enriched soil. Here, instead, nothing showed, and until it was imported from other areas, nothing ever would.

For the warheads used had been of two types: the heavy, crater-making bombs that flatten cities, whose crushing effects were visible for kilometers in all directions; and the enhanced radiation weapons that produce thousands of megaroentgens of hard radiation and slow neutrons. The effects of the former were obvious. Under that barrage, the city was as effectively demolished as it would have been if the world's sun had been momentarily brought to its surface. The effects of the latter form of weapon were short-term. Within hours after their detonation the area was safe for occupation by soldiers in protective outfits; within two days, even the outfits were no longer needed. It didn't matter. No soldiers lived. No songbirds lived either, nor earthworms, nor bacteria. The trees were dead, the flowering plants were dead, and even the buried grass seeds could not survive.

As he headed north, Tyler left the zone of destruction of one large warhead and entered another. The city had been too large for any one weapon available to this world. The sight, and the knowledge, numbed him, signalling an end to his rage and his misery. Once again he had passed through the triple cycle that so marred his life: violent emotion; a sick contrition; and a numb tiredness, an aching coldness.

He saw the endless rows of bent-over houses and buildings, and the lifeless, burnt-out terrain, as if through thick glass. There was an artificial distance between him and what he could see, and this distance was inside his head.

Finally, to his relief, he left that area of the city and flew north at top speed. At the boundary of the radiation warheads' kill-zone, a sparse and patchy growth of grass began, turning within a few kilometers into neatly laid-out hectares of farmland, seemingly untouched by the destruction. But no farmers tended the regular pastures, and no herds of farm animals survived. They had been the casualties of the first wave of survivors leaving the corpse of the city. When these people, now homeless and desperate, had come across food stockpiles and herd animals, with only a few half-organized groups of farmers to protect themselves, a slaughter had ensued. Within six days, all the food animals were gone; within another two days, the entire food stockpile of the area was depleted. The horde—or such of it that yet lived—moved on.

Five weeks, Tyler knew, was a very long time for homeless, desperate people. All civilized restraints were gone, leaving only one overruling concept: survival. Five weeks was easily long enough for an atomic age civilization to revert to the old stone age.

He flew north, leaving behind him all evidence of the disaster. At sundown he flew lazy spirals over a promising campsite; surprising no occupants, he landed the helicopter and made his camp for the night.

*   *   *

Morning was no more than a lightening of the heavily overcast sky. Although no rain had fallen, the angry gray of the thick cloud cover suggested that rain might not be far off. Tyler knew that the atmosphere was overloaded with dust and heavy particles raised from the many explosions over the continent. Despite this, when he looked out over the endless, brooding landscape, he felt as though nature itself mourned the waste and the death.

He glanced about the small camp, and, seeing nothing to interest him further, packed his belongings and tossed them aboard the helicopter. It struck him that no living being might ever again visit this spot, and drink out of the small stream that slid over the ice-rimmed rocks. At once the chill sank deeply into him, and it was with a sense of relief that he clambered into the helicopter, there to switch on its interior heater. Minutes later he was travelling north again over the outstretched wasteland.

His plans were sketchy, but seemed reasonable to him. Quite a way to the north was a series of advance rescue camps manned by volunteers from Horlan cities, from the Concordat, and from the many wandering bands of local survivors. The camps, in turn, had thrown out scattered substations to directly help the starving and homeless people wherever they might have taken root. Tyler intended to go directly to the substation nearest the ruins of Vis city and, under some pretense, head north into the wilderness. He expected his hunt to last only a week or two. Protected by two pistols and a heavy rifle, he had no fear of looters or brigands.

A guide, he had decided, would be necessary. Payment would be easily arranged, and against betrayal he had his own quick wit and fast draw to rely upon. Hiring a guide did not mean letting him in on his plans for assassination, however, and while that limited Tyler's freedom of action slightly, he was quite confident in his ability to complete the mission.

On the third day he arrived at advance camp Epsilon, where his presence was greeted rather stormily.

"Back off, boys. Nothing for us here." The voice belonged to the stout man who had pulled open the cargo hatch of the helicopter the moment the machine was settled on the beaten-earth landing pad at camp Epsilon.

"What d'ye mean? No provisions? Nothing?"

"Three bags, and they're his."

Tyler gazed dispassionately over the small crowd of angry men, not particularly heeding their anger. His fighting pistol was within easy reach, holstered under his left arm, but from his long experience at reading crowds, he doubted he would need it.

A spokesman for the group appointed himself, thrusting his face through the open helicopter hatch. "Your cargo compartment," he said reasonably, "is empty. Why would that be?"

"Because I'm not here to ferry cargo. I'm here for a look-about, so I can report to the higher-ups on how things go here."

The man, a large, florid type who hadn't shaven since the bombs fell, brushed his chin on his sleeve and looked coolly at Tyler. "You might have loaded up a few bales of supplies, you know. Deliveries out here are irregular, and what we have more of than anything else is shortages."

Tyler leaned forward to swing out of the saddle. The man stepped back. "Divide the shortages equally. Fair's fair." He turned his back on the muttering pack and drew two of his suitcases from the space behind the pilot's seat. Eyeing the quiet, angry group, he pointed to one of the smaller men and ordered peremptorily, "Show me to some place where I can sleep undisturbed." Guessing that he could safely wring the tension one notch tighter, he added, "Don't you people have anything useful to go and do?"

Cold silence greeted this remark. On top of the disappointment caused by the false hope of provisions, Tyler's attitude was just shy of intolerable. But Tyler had judged his audience well. Quietly, their wrath merely simmering, the men stomped off through the frost-lined campground.

Finally, Tyler was alone with the man he'd tagged, and with the first man, who seemed uninterested in leaving. Instead, he turned to face Tyler and said, somewhat harshly, "Name's Garvey. Fulmer Garvey. What exactly is your business here?"

Tyler regarded him icily. Garvey turned to the other man and gestured.

The man left.

"You're not held in the best odor here, and you've been here less than fifteen minutes," Garvey continued. "If you want to be let alone, you'd best give me a story to pass around."

"You seem like a well-educated man, Mr. Garvey. Why are you playing king of the pond?"

Garvey smiled. "I was indeed well-educated. Switching circuits. And it wasn't war work, either." His smile disappeared. "You from Horla?"

"Farther."

"Off-planet, then. Around here, don't ever accuse a man of war work. I was in telephone switching, and I'll spike the man that says otherwise."

"Whatever you say, of course," Tyler said easily. His expression gave the lie to his smooth words.

"You, I can't figure," Garvey said after a moment. "In you drop, without even the common courtesy of bringing a load of the supplies we desperately need." He looked away. "They've got bales of stuff for us; they've got tons of it. You came all this way with an empty cargo compartment."

"Unless you like freezing, I suggest we move along. It's been a long day."

Garvey made no answer to that, but rather continued in his previous vein. "Then, once we're all already offended, you lash out with what were close to fighting words."

"Are you offering to fight me?" Tyler knew damned well that Garvey was not.

"Who are you, and why are you here?"

"That's none of your business."

"That's always understood. You say it's none of my business, and I agree. That out of the way, who are you, and why are you here?"

Tyler began to feel a liking for the man. "I'm James Tyler, Commander, Concordat Navy. I'm here—"

"Name of three dead gods!" Garvey swore. "Our planetary charter says we're free of you and your damned green flag. What in hell are you doing here cluttering up the landscape?"

"Instead of us standing here freezing, let's walk, and I'll tell you."

Garvey was agreeable. They set off on an informal tour of the camp, Garvey in the lead, Tyler working to keep up with the heavier man's stride.

"The Concordat is looking into incorporating this world, on the rationale that you've proven yourselves unfit for independence."

Garvey spat, and made no reply. Tyler used the long silence that followed to look about.

Laid out north-to-south, the camp consisted of several dozen low, prefabricated buildings, all snow-capped and windowless. In the center stood two older, prewar buildings, constructed of wood and dressed stone. Now, in the gathering dark, lights shone in the windows of these houses. Dinner was nearing; men and women filed into the buildings; smoke coiled from cobblestone chimneys, spreading a sharp scent over the downwind half of the camp.

Tyler could see the trenches where workers had labored to build a backup drainage and sewage system. Patches of gardens had been ploughed behind each hut, although nothing grew yet to reward the effort. An unfinished rock wall divided a field. To the east was visible a shallow quarry where the flat fieldstones were pried up from the frozen earth.

Much of it was makework, Tyler guessed: cold, hard labor to keep the people that straggle in from the hills tired, happy, and honest. They may be handing out

free food here, he thought, but the last thing they
want is a prefabricated welfare class. This early in the
recovery, and this low in the foothills, raids from organized pillagers were not to be feared.

The thought gave Tyler a conversational opening.
"Garvey?"

"Hm?"

"Which do you resent more: the Concordat, or Horlan
opportunists?"

Garvey thought. "I see what you're saying, and I
can't disagree. When we settled this world, and got
our freedom, we backslid a bit in our technology. We
lost the power, economically, to build our own spaceships, and had to learn a lot of the tricks from the
beginning, especially of running an entire planet. The
Concordat offered no gifts, and we asked for none. We
were free men.

"Well, we mucked up, badly; and presto, there's the
Concordat, with their free aid, and a big rescue effort,
with all the usual strings attached.

"But it seems to me that at least the Horlans are of
our own stock. I've got family over on Horla, and if
maybe they wouldn't have been so quick with the
canned food, at least they'd be offering it for free.

"Would the Concordat preserve the old national
boundaries? Or would we turn into the United Theury
Province? I'm from Vistheur; so are most of the people
in this camp. Maybe our grudge against Saftheur was
idiotic. Given hindsight, it seems that way. Well, the
argument is gone, but the differences remain."

Tyler walked beside the man silently, his feet crunch-
ing a path through the untrodden ice. To his surprise,
they had wandered beyond the camp, and were now
straying down the gentle slope toward a muddy stream.

There was to be no repetition of the scene he had
caused in Commander Denis's office; he was not in
that frame of mind. To get his man, to go back to
somewhere warm, were his only concerns. This cold,
cheerless land had gotten into his mind, and he wanted
to be done with it.

They arrived at last at the bank of the small, swift stream that supplied fresh water to the camp. Garvey stared into the icy swiftness and at the rock-strewn bottom. Tyler watched Garvey.

"I'm going to be travelling up-country," the assassin said, at last coming to business. "I'll need a good guide."

"I'm your man, then," Garvey answered without hesitation.

"Aren't you too busy bossing it here?"

"Me? The boss? Whatever gave you that idea? The most you could call me is the foreman. Big Jacob is the boss."

It was by now almost too dark for the two men to see each other. The stream rushed pleasantly behind them.

"So you can be spared here for a week or so?"

Garvey thought. "Yeah, I think so. What's the pay?"

"I can get you a portable electric generator, nuclear pack, variable output. Um . . . I don't have it on me, of course—"

"Your word's good enough for me. With one of those, I'd be fairly popular around here, and in short order. Deal."

"We'll leave in the morning. An hour before sunrise."

"Fine. I'll look forward to coming back and ousting whatever punk has risen to foreman in my absence."

The two strode back to the camp. A sentry, well-bundled against the bitter cold, hailed them. Garvey cursed him sourly, and that settled that.

After dinner, which consisted mostly of canned stuff, and which was only grudgingly offered to Tyler at all, he and Garvey squared the trip with Big Jacob.

Big Jacob was true to his name. By as much as Garvey outweighed Tyler, Jacob McGinnis outweighed Garvey. He had a wrestler's build, and his low forehead and small eyes lent him an appearance of imbecility which he dispelled only with difficulty. His five-weeks' beard was at least clean, his manner of dress dignified, and his speech precise, clear, and articulate. His first words were, unfortunately, in the nature of a blunder.

"So this is our most recent benefactor! Thanks for the cargo-load of provisions. Shame they couldn't have lasted longer."

Tyler clutched at his self-control like a falling man at a safety railing. His wrath churned, warm and inviting.

"My mission is more important than any ferry-run, Mr. McGinnis. It affects the whole future of this planet."

McGinnis's eyebrows rose. "And how might that be?"

Once again Tyler gave his cover story; once again it proved to be an unpopular idea.

"Our planetary charter guarantees us our independence for as long as we wish it," McGinnis snapped. Garvey nodded, remaining, however, a spectator to the debate.

"It seems that that particular document burned when Vis city was exploded," Tyler purred, a dangerous light glinting behind his eyes. "Can we still consider it a valid contract?"

"Copies exist on Horla continent." McGinnis drank from the great stein at his elbow. "Nothing in the document has been invalidated by the war."

"Its preamble, I believe, said something to the effect that independence was to assure self-determination 'For us and our progeny, that our lives shall be the richer.' " The sarcasm rose easily to his tongue. "Just how much richer is your life?"

McGinnis said nothing. He watched Tyler with a terrible patience that the latter found far more unnerving than he would have found open resentment.

Tyler's flames beat higher. "If this world had had a sane and workable planetary government, perhaps independence would have meant something. The difference between Saftheur and Vistheur would not have been lost, but would have been impartially arbitrated. Now both Saftheur and Vistheur are dead, gentlemen, and the first boatloads of Horlans are already loading up."

"You have some valid points. A world government— elected by us, not imposed upon us!—might have prevented the madness. How, on the other hand, could a government-in-occupation, devised by the Concordat, address itself to our special needs?"

"Your special needs are at this moment radioactive dust floating high in a dark and stormy sky!" Tyler shook himself, and seemed to come fully alive for the first time in several days.

"Hindsight apart, and ignoring the fact that it's much too late, consider: Even as it is, you've got Concordat protection, whether you like it or not. This world is well within our sphere of concern. Should another star-faring race covet it, it would be our Navy and our ground forces that would defend you. Thus, the billions that you spent on weapons and armies was useful only against others on your own planet.

"That means billions not put into your economy. Worse yet, by not plugging yourselves smoothly into the overall Concordat economy, you guarantee waste and useless duplication of effort. On top of that, by dividing into twenty-odd economic provinces planetwide, your total wastage becomes exorbitant. Over ninety percent of your economy was purely and simply wasted."

"If our wastage was that large, don't you think our profit-makers would have urged merger with the Concordat? They're reasonable men." McGinnis spoke in smooth, calming tones.

Tyler was beginning to feel the sickness that would take him after a furious burst of anger, after he'd taken a foe apart with his best well-placed curses. The argument was useless—everyone had his mind made up; no one would listen. Willingly he'd drop it right now and retire, but for purposes of artistic reality, he had no choice but to follow it out.

"Where do you think all that waste money ended up? In your wise, benevolent, altruistic profit-makers' pockets! In *your* case: what tax rate did you pay?"

McGinnis shrugged. "Ten to twelve percent on all income."

"Under a unified planetary economy, that can be reduced to two per cent without loss of real public benefits. The same is true of property taxes. Most of what you were paying went to arms manufacturers, contractors, and to the soldiers themselves. It—"

"You're lucky we're in a closed room, Mr. Tyler. I don't mind this discussion; neither does Garvey. Bring this up in public, and I'll see you torn apart. The bottom line: I don't mind the idea of a planetary government, given certain guarantees of local freedom. But I will not accept a foreign takeover, such as you propose. The freedom of my country comes first."

That did it. "You were in war work, weren't you." Tyler swept his hand across the table, knocking the stein to the floor. "You have a personal interest in division, hatred, war. How many cities did you destroy? How many children did you fry?"

Garvey backed away from the table, leaving McGinnis a clear approach to Tyler. McGinnis's eyes closed to slits. "I was *not* in war work. But I worked for a strong Vistheur, to keep her free of foreign domination."

Tyler gestured around the room, taking in, by implication, the camp, the hills, and the entire wasted continent. "Strong, eh?" His ice-gray eyes bored into McGinnis's small black ones.

Ultimately, it was McGinnis's greater physical power that prevented a fight. He knew, with an ironclad certainty, that he could take this Tyler and tie him in knots. Because he had no need to prove it, he was the first to turn away. Bending down, he retrieved the stein, which by odd chance had not broken. He turned to Garvey.

"Do you want to go with him?"

Almost apologetically, Garvey spread his hands. "I'm getting paid."

"Fine. I'll see you when you return." He stood, ending the conversation, and left the room.

"Tomorrow," Tyler said to Garvey in a low voice. His mind churned with images of McGinnis; he'd never before met a man with the self-possession to refuse his invitation. Tyler had no doubt: He could have taken McGinnis and destroyed him. Strength counted for much, but skill for a great deal more.

He'd met three people with three different reasons for wanting planetary independence. No two of them agreed, and yet all three were in agreement. In a quiet foyer, he donned his jacket. Garvey followed him into the darkness. Tyler nodded a good-night to him, and stalked back to his cabin. His sleep was deep and dreamless.

An hour before sunrise he woke, and was dressed in time to answer Garvey's knock. Within three minutes the helicopter was loaded and ready. The morning's chill quiet was shattered by the roar of the rotors. The machine fell away into the sky, its engine noise fading off into the north.

In Exonidas city the rain fell steadily as it had for two days. The streets of the vice district were dark, and the street lights did little to dispel the gloom.

No customers were likely to wander into Lady Titania's on a day as unpleasant as this, and the girls who lived on the premises found the time pressing upon them heavily.

Glory paced, catlike, from window to door and back. Sylvia munched on the sandwich she held in one hand, while reading a slick magazine that she gripped in the other. Jill sat curled in a chair by the heat register, her eyes focussed on infinity.

At the window, Glory stopped and peered out. "Beastly weather."

"When's the headmistress going to be back?" Jill asked. Sylvia glanced up, only to bury herself in her magazine again.

"Oh, she phoned in, a couple of hours ago," Glory said, pacing. "She's staying home. We can have the day free."

"Sounds good."

They resumed their time-passing pursuits.

On the rear cover of the magazine that Sylvia held tightly gripped in her left hand, a large yellow and blue advertisement caught Jill's eye. The number '17' was visible between Sylvia's fingers.

Cubicle seventeen, Jill thought; a blond man with gray eyes. He'd kissed her, roughly and intimately, and without permission—but she hadn't really minded. She put up with worse daily; she had since she was seventeen. He'd been unlike the others, though. When she'd kissed him back, he'd withdrawn, embarrassed. Who was he? Perhaps Glory would remember his name . . .

"Whose?"

"Was I thinking aloud?" Jill asked, seeing both Glory and Sylvia watching her.

"Two days in this place with no customers, with nothing to listen to but the rain on the roof, and we're lucky we're not all talking to ourselves." Glory turned to stare out the window again. "Who were you thinking of?"

"The tall, slim, blond one who came a few days ago to use cubicle seventeen."

Sylvia laid down her magazine. Glory turned and sat lithely on the floor by the window, gazing at Jill.

"I've wondered about him. He pinched my ear. It hurt, too."

"He swatted me. Jill got the best from him."

"Yes. She did. What about him?"

"Well," Jill began, strangely shy, "we don't know anything about him. What does he do in there? What is his name?"

Glory tossed herself to her feet and started across the room for the door. "Let's go find out. The key's downstairs."

Sylvia was off her couch in a moment, enlivened by the prospect of doing anything other than read that magazine through again. "I'm with you."

Jill felt a momentary reservation, until she looked again at her two friends. They were caught up in the idea of opening cubicle seventeen, prying into it like a hidden gift. It took Jill a moment before she was able to admit that she, too, felt more than merely idly curious. "Let's go." If anything went wrong, at least she could leave these two with the blame.

Downstairs, at the headmistress' desk, Glory sorted through the keys, immediately finding the one to cubicle seventeen. She darted off down the corridor, but was recalled by a call from Sylvia.

"I've found the appointment book, Jill, Glory. Here, for that day, noon. Cubicle seventeen: James Tyler."

"That won't be his real name," Glory objected.

"Maybe not, but it's something." Jill found the name comforting. When something unknown has a name, she had discovered, it loses much of its power over one.

At the door to cubicle seventeen they paused again, Glory and Sylvia for the first time acutely aware of the wrong they intended. "What the hell," Glory tossed in, and bent to the door with the key.

Without her having pressed the hidden catch by the doorknob, the key activated the cutoff switch in the message transmitter that was the wooden table in the room. By the time the three girls had opened the door and peered within, the table was no more than what it seemed, and would never be again.

"An empty room?"

"With a table?"

"He comes in here and plays with himself," Sylvia snickered. Jill frowned.

"He writes things?" Glory said, unsure.

"He meets someone?" Sylvia piped. A quick look around the room dispelled that possibility. There was only the one door, and all three of them had stood near it for Tyler's full hour inside.

While the others played at being detectives, peering under the table and into all the corners, Jill stood in the doorway. She slowly realized that they would never find anything suspicious. The secrets of this room— and she was firmly convinced that there were secrets here—would not be easily discovered.

By the time they had tired of poking about the featureless and unrewarding room, night had fallen. Glory announced, in tones that made it clear she felt the day to have been totally wasted, that she was going to bed and did not care to be disturbed. Sylvia

took up her magazine, and, fighting great yawns, went
to work on the word-search.

Jill went off to her bed to try to sleep, but passed the
night uneasily. Tyler's image hovered at the edge of
her dreams, laughing sardonically. In the morning she
couldn't remember whether he had threatened her, or
she had threatened him. It was only a dream, anyway;
wasn't it?

The rain did not relent. Faced with another day of
monotony, the three girls agreed to lock the place up
and scatter, to try to find some diverting way to pass
the time.

Jill, in raincoat and large floppy hat, found herself
walking aimlessly down the drenched streets, looking
without interest into shop windows. At a public phone
kiosk she stopped and keyed the directory. There was
no entry for James Tyler, although one J. Tyler was
listed. Almost, she gave up and left. Gripped by the
impulse of the moment, however, she punched in the
number. After a moment, a woman's voice answered.

"Hello?"

"Uh, hello. Is James Tyler there?"

"I'm sorry; the only Tyler here is me."

"May I ask . . . ?"

"No. I'm sorry, I don't know any James Tyler. I'm
Jasmina, and I'm single. My father's name is Tomas. I
can't help you."

"Thank you."

The connection was broken.

It was pointless, she thought. It couldn't be his real
name. He was using an alias . . .

That didn't satisfy her either. Blast it, he *looked* like
a James Tyler. People often—no, nearly always—looked
like their names, in her experience. Nearly always.

A thought struck her. Maybe he was from off-planet,
with the rescue volunteers. Again, she almost gave
the effort up, but found that she really wanted to
know. There had been something about him that
charged her, that intrigued her. She had to know.

Without waiting further, she phoned the Concordat Consulate, located in the spaceport terminal.

A voice, filtered by a poor connection, identified the Consulate and asked her business.

"I'm looking for a man named James Tyler. He may be with the volunteer rescue mission."

"One moment."

Soon another voice came on the line. It was a man's voice, deep and laden with undertones. "May I help you?"

Jill repeated her query.

"Hm. Let me check . . . That would be Commander James Tyler of the Concordat Navy. He's on a fact-finding mission to Theury continent, and we don't know when he'll be back. Can I take a message?"

Jill thought swiftly, and could think of nothing that would pass. "No, I guess not."

"Thank you, ma'am."

She broke the connection and walked back out into the pouring rain. For several minutes she walked at random, ignoring the people about her. Finally, determination seized her. There was still ample time. It was meaningless, she chided herself; it was foolish and wasteful. But despite her self-criticism, her feet carried her swiftly forward, over the rain-slick sidewalks.

Leaving the vice district, Jill passed through the business and banking district, making her way at last to the speedramp approach that would carry her quickly the short distance to the spaceport. She could already see its towering fuel tanks on the horizon by the bay.

The city unfolded itself below her as the express slide crossed midtown on the high rail. The rain splashed at her, and she huddled in her raincoat, trying to ignore it. The city descended to the bay, its character changing as the different districts became visible. Jill saw the beauty of it as if for the first time, and the knowledge that cities fully as beautiful across the Sea of Lamps had been burned utterly away heightened her appreciation of this gem, this thing so precious that it must be protected. No one who saw any city with the awareness she found now could ever order a warhead fired.

The speedramp crested, dropped rapidly toward the gigantic spaceport terminal complex, and entered a long above-ground tunnel. When that opened up, she was inside the five-story terminal building, at the slide and tram station, high at the end of the east wing. Not far from where she stood, a large window gave an aspect of the outdoor gravitic boost-grid that was the heart of the port itself. Over it the gray skies dropped their everlasting veil of rain; in the windless weather the rainfall was slow and vertical.

As she watched, a Navy shuttle dropped into sight, being lowered by gravitic forces emanating from the powerful grid. Dropping toward a point just off the grid itself, the shuttle was lowered gracefully. The grid maneuvered it, manipulated it as if by a huge, invisible hand, placing it softly on a target pad.

Jill sensed someone standing by her, watching also. She half-turned. The gentleman met her glance.

"Quite a sight, eh, ma'am? I never get tired of it."

He was tall, beefy, tanned, with dark hair and a wide, never-ending smile. His whole face smiled, as if at a very good joke. Jill had him sized up in less time than it took for her to turn away. And she turned away invitingly.

"I've never been here before," she said, and she didn't need to over-act. The man was wearing the uniform and rank-medallion of a Navy Lieutenant Commander, and he was interested in her. What more could she need?

"Well, the landing's the same from place to place, but each world is different, and that makes everything different. It's raining now; earlier in your year it probably snowed. I expect you saw how the field had trapped some of the raindrops 'round the shuttle, giving it a sort of halo. That's a real nice effect in falling snow."

Inwardly, Jill exulted. The fact that he was patient and clever enough to use poetic imagery rather than a straightforward line, showed that he was the sort of man upon whom her strategems would best succeed. *Give me an officer over an enlisted man any day,* she thought. She'd been a prostitute so long, she'd forgotten what it was to be tactfully wooed. It was pleasant, being reminded.

She looked up at him again, giving the impression of having just noticed his uniform. "You're Navy, aren't you?"

He laughed, gently, easily. "Yes, ma'am."

"Perhaps you could help me."

To say that he tensed would be inaccurate; rather, he became, without giving any sign whatever, more alert. The little doors behind his eyes prepared to slam shut, while still giving this strange and attractive young woman the benefit of the doubt.

"In what way, ma'am?"

"Well," she managed to look both embarrassed and urgent at the same time. "Two young Navy officers saved me from the attentions of an inebriated sloven in a restaurant several days ago. I was able to catch the name of one of them—James Tyler—and I hoped to be able to track them down and thank them. I think the other's name was Albert something; he was trim, with brown hair, blue eyes . . ." She trailed off, giving exactly the impression she wanted. Her companion discerned that it was Tyler's friend, 'Albert,' that this young lovely actually wanted to meet again, because she had, on that short encounter, developed an attachment for him.

He couldn't know that Jill had invented 'Albert' on the spot; he couldn't resist the temptation of playing the game, and competing with Albert for the young woman's attention.

"Well, I'll see what I can do." He wiped his hand, and held it out. "My name's Richard Temple, Concordat Navy."

Jill took his hand as would a lady of the better class. "Jill Imfarland. Pleased to meet you."

"Pleasure's mine, ma'am." He turned and gestured toward a stopped spaceport shuttle bus. Once aboard, he explained, "This'll take us to the Navy base, where maybe I'll pull a little rank, and find out what you want." He thought for a time, as the crowded corridors slid past.

"James Tyler, eh? Here with the rescue mission?"

"I'm afraid I don't know—may I call you Richard?"

"Certainly—Jill."

Things were looking good for both of them.

Much later that night, when she was at last alone, Jill knew the following things about James Tyler: he was thirty years old, single, of unknown parentage and homeworld; he was a Commander in the Support Branch of the Navy, here on a mission to determine whether the world should be merged into the Concordat. Currently he was at an unknown location in the wilds of Theury continent, there by what Richard Temple had described as: "Strangely imprecise orders, cut somewhere higher up."

Jill knew one other thing about James Tyler: she loved him. His face laughed, winked, grinned, cheerfully, embarrassedly, through her mind's eye; his kiss was ever hot upon her lips. As much as she tried to shake herself away from what she knew to be a childish infatuation, she was unable to clear him from her mind.

I know nothing of him. Nothing. He may be a boor, a bastard, an absolutely despicable thug. I've got to be realistic about this.

She could not.

Temple had been quite helpful; he'd been attentive, correct, charming; by buying her a fine dinner, he'd easily met her price. She admired him a great deal, but it was nevertheless true that an evening in bed with him had not excited her as much as one impulsive kiss from James Tyler.

Eventually she was able to sleep. In her dreams Tyler came to her. They did not make love, but instead sat at the side of a grassy riverbank and spoke sadly, longingly, on a topic that Jill, in the morning, was unable to remember.

*   *   *

Voices in the office of Security Director Peter Anthony, the man to whom Richard Temple was temporarily assigned:

"All of it public information, of course."

"Of course."

"I did what I thought best—"

"Calm yourself; calm yourself. Of course you did right. You've been well-trained, and your training came through."

"In that case . . ."

"Yes?"

"What is it with this James Tyler?"

"I don't know any more than you do or she does. After you've left, I'll look up what the code means."

"It can't be terribly secret, exposed the way it was on his transcript."

"Ah, but it could be. That seven-digit notation could mean anything. All I know is that we know something about James Tyler that isn't meant to be public knowledge."

"Well, she didn't get any such."

"I never said that she did. Why are you so defensive?"

"Sorry, sir."

"Relax. Who could she be working for that would want information on a Navy Commander?"

"Your world doesn't really have any organized crime."

"No. We swept them away for once and for all. My predecessor in this office had his hands full, but he triumphed."

"What about the illegal political splinter groups?"

"There are those . . ."

"I'm thinking specifically of the Planetary Independence Party."

"Hm. Them. Damned nuisance. I'd like to have them all arrested."

"I've begun to think that they're more than merely a nuisance, sir. I think they're a menace. Most of their members are common laborers, but they recruit among gamblers, thugs, and others who are very close to criminals."

"I've studied them—"

"Then you know the danger they pose. They've vowed to clear the Concordat from this world, by force if necessary. They were implicated in the attempted bombing at the east gate."

"That? That was a botched job from the start."

"Nevertheless, it proves their intent, and their fanatacism; I've fought insurrectionists—'counterrevolutionaries'—before."

"Have you?"

"I had to have this eye regrown after the dawn raid at Pryde field. I won't forget."

"Calm yourself. Even I've heard of Pryde field. Our local troublemakers are simply not in that league."

"Perhaps. But I won't take that chance."

"Well . . . What do we know about this mysterious woman who asked these unauthorized questions?"

"She said her name was Jill Imfarland."

"Imfarland? Let's check the directory . . . Ha. There it is: her real name. Is that her face?"

"Yes. That's her."

"She can't be terribly dangerous if she uses her real name. However . . . let's see what the big file has on her . . . Nothing. Maybe the police file has something."

"You have the local police file on access?"

"Certainly. That's the big advantage to being a local man. If I were Concordat, I'd need to go through channels. It'd take time . . . There she is. Jill Imfarland: known prostitute."

"What!?"

"I thought that might take you by surprise. Did you and she . . . ?"

"Yes. Damn it, I thought she—"

"I see."

"How could she have . . ."

"Enough of that. What about this 'Albert' she asked after?"

"Not enough information. Sorry about the outburst, sir."

"It was to be expected. She'd led you on. Very well;

we need to know who her control is, for whom she is working, and so on. I'll leave that to you. I'll research this James Tyler, and work on it from that angle."

"Yes, sir."

"Very good, then, Temple. I'll see you . . . tomorrow, eh?"

Richard Temple—Lieutenant Commander, Concordat Navy, Intelligence Branch—fumed as he walked through the corridors of the Naval Base of the Exonidas Spaceport. Perhaps he hadn't exactly been betrayed, he forcefully reminded himself, and, yes, he had gotten his full satisfaction from the little tart. It still stung him that he had been so completely fooled. Thinking with one's glands, rather than with one's supposedly well-trained brain, was a sure way of courting complications. Now his emotions were all tied up in the matter, confusing the real issues of just who was spying upon whom, and why.

The Concordat had no shortage of enemies, both in the interstellar arena and here, locally, among the dissatisfied of this world. They seemed irrationally touchy about their independence, and the attitude puzzled Temple. The benefits of full Concordat membership outweighed the drawbacks by an incredible proportion. Surely, somewhere in their great store of documents, the Concordat's Praesidium had a planetary charter tailored to preserve this world's illusion of freedom. Pull a constitution like that from their file, fill in this world's name in the blank spaces, and have some duly-elected fool slap his signature to it. Instantly, a viable and contributive world has added itself to the Concordat. There was no one else in this region of space with whom to trade anyway. Why not make it legal?

Instead, there were many who insisted that the old treaty be honored, even when its terms had been clearly contradicted by the recent planet-maiming war. Most vociferous among these was the Planetary Independence Party. Before now, they might have been no more than speechmakers and publishers of one-page scrap sheets. Temple felt a growing alarm at their current activities. What could they want with information on James Tyler? Did they intend to lobby him, to influence his final report to the Navy?

According to the file, Tyler was investigating planetary independence. That was the only reason that the planet's restive, nearly rebellious "freedom fighters" might be interested in him. But, Temple reminded himself, he didn't know nearly enough about that elusive and slightly suspicious Commander Tyler; there might be more involved here than was evident.

Temple needed to find out.

Later, from his apartment, he began his inquiries by phone. Jill Imfarland's name was listed in the directory, and a number, but no address. Nodding sagely, Temple made the connection.

"Hello?"

"Hello, Jill? This is Richard. Richard Temple. I thought it would be nice if we could meet again."

"Oh." She recovered swiftly; so swiftly that if Temple hadn't been paying close attention and listening for it, he would have missed her brief hesitation.

"I'd love to meet you again, Richard. I . . ."

"Yes?"

"I don't know whether or not I should apologize for my behavior last night. I . . ."

You were strictly professional, my dear. "I guess I should be the one to apologize. I rather took advantage of you, and . . ."

"Still, I don't usually do . . . what we did."

You don't say, slut. You're not a bad actress, though. "Since we both enjoyed ourselves, and no harm was done, then there's no point in worrying, is there? I think no less of you, and so . . . are you free this afternoon?"

"Yes, I am."

"Shall I drop by to pick you up?"

"My place is in no condition to be seen . . . Can I meet you?"

No less than I expected, from someone who lives in a bordello named 'Lady Titania's.' No, I guess it wouldn't be fit to be seen. "How about Wrokla's—downtown, Laurel and 5th—my treat."

"I'd be delighted. Half an hour?"

"Fine."

He disconnected, and phoned Director Anthony at the spaceport.

"Sir?"

"Yes?"

"Richard Temple here. Have you learned anything that you can tell me . . . about James Tyler?"

"This isn't a safe line, you know."

"I'm calling from my apartment, as you said to. I think I'd find a bug if one were here to be found."

"Hm. Very well. James Tyler is an assassin. That took me every last one of my security clearances to discover, and you know how well I'm trusted. I don't know who his target is, or who his control is. There's indication that he receives his assignment through some sort of double-blind called the Black Book."

"Whose side is he on?"

"Well, I have to assume it's ours. The file doesn't say, in so many words."

"And we don't know why this Jill Imfarland is after him?"

"Her file is—or was—clear as a bell, save for some local whoring. I've updated it to include our suspicions. Have you set up an appointment with her?"

"Yes. I'm meeting her shortly."

"I don't need to emphasize how important this might be. You'll be on your own discretion. We need to know for whom she is working, and what her assignment is."

"I'll do my best, sir."

"I know you will."

Wrokla's was perhaps the finest restaurant in the city and, although the proposition was sometimes debated, the management relied heavily upon it in their publicity. It was a great complex occupying the top three floors of an otherwise uninteresting building just across the business district from the vice district.

Jill had never been there before, having been excluded by her low station, not by lack of cash. At the elevator door a strong, brusque gentleman asked her her business. Taken aback, she mentioned that she was waiting for her companion. The gentleman gestured absently to a lounge where she might wait in some comfort. With that, he faded back into the overhanging plants and ferns, presumably to pounce upon the next unwary diner.

Through an open-work screen, Jill could see a portion of the actual dining room. It was cunningly laid out on artistically descending and ascending platforms, so that no more than a small part of the room was visible from any other part. Each table, on the other hand, had a spectacular view of the city spread out below. Jill could overlook her own neighborhood. From this high vantage, it looked utterly insignificant: a colorful speck in a sea of buildings. Gaudy flashing lights and garish signboards were diminished by distance to firefly flickers of dim light. Beyond, the city descended toward the great hooked bay, at the north point of which the spaceport lay, just out of Jill's field of vision.

Finally, Richard Temple arrived, brushed off the doorman with a tactless ease that Jill found quite refreshing, and strode in to greet her. She rose, took his hands, and gave him a restrained lover's kiss.

"Perhaps the couple would care for a table?" The unctuous doorman had pursued them, even into the sanctuary of the lounge.

"They would," Temple said in a chill tone.

"You may follow me," the doorman magnanimously granted them, and led them toward another overly solicitous gentleman, who, it was to be presumed, would lead them to the man who would finally seat them.

That ritual accomplished, punctuated at each exchange of dignitary by a tasteful—that is, small—

gratuity from Temple, the two found themselves seated
at a small table with an acceptable view. The table sat
uncomfortably close to a joining of two arching metal
beams, unsuccessfully disguised by a row of flowering
plants. They were in the portion of the seating that
was reserved for the cheap and the indigent: the sort
of people that just might order steak and potatoes
without shame.

Temple surprised them, if that was what they expected. Not only was he able to order and to afford a
well-thought-out meal from the local gourmet reper-
toire, but he ordered it without flaw in the affected
tones of the local subdialect, which measured one's
status as a sophisticated diner. Suddenly it became
the error of the maître d' that he had misread *Sieur*
Temple's behavior and had relegated him to the status
of *peon*. Lost thereby was the magnificent tip that
ordinarily would be forthcoming, to be split fairly between the maître d' and the management. Probably
the good sir's patronage was as well lost . . . but excel-
lent service and properly prepared food might—partially—restore his good will.

The meal was the best that Jill had ever tasted. As
much as she enjoyed it, she knew that she was missing
many of the subtleties of the language of spices and
essences, simply from her unfamiliarity with such craft.
The wine that followed dinner was crisp, gentle, and
fragrant. Since her previous experience with alcohol
had been limited to smelling it on the hot breath of
her clients—no one was going to force her to actually
drink that street-vintage trash—she found herself
quickly dizzied by the quiet, yet potent, quality wine
with which Temple plied her.

As yet, all she suspected that he wanted from her
was another night in bed. *Any more of this stuff, and
I'll be asleep the moment I'm horizontal. He might like
it that way, but I doubt that it would be quite the same.*

Over coffee, Temple began to fish for information.
This was his primary goal, which he would not let
stand in the way of his getting "that Imfarland slut"

into the sack for a second night. Now that he knew what she was, he found that he still enjoyed and desired her services.

"I couldn't find out anything more about that James Tyler. I don't know when he'll be back from Theury continent. Do you still need to see him?"

Even slightly inebriated, Jill retained enough caution to answer that one properly. "Since I've met you, finding that Albert person seems . . . less important. It just seems that it's something I should do."

"To thank him properly?"

"You make it sound so trivial. I'm sure I should forget it all. But . . ."

"But what?"

She shook her head, whatever she had been about to say lost in an alcoholic haze.

"Jill, if you're covering for something more important, can't you trust me? Surely you know that I have only your best interests in mind."

Jill hovered between hysterical giggling and tears of sorrow. It was as great a struggle as she had ever waged, to keep the roiling emotions that filled her from overwhelming her. Unused to strong drink, she couldn't be certain whether it was mere alcohol that so affected her, or a stronger drug that Temple had mixed in with the already potent beverage. She had no firm reason to suspect the latter, and so dismissed the notion with an effort.

"Of course I trust you, Richard. It was no more than a romantic game, a child's quest. I wanted to follow the more handsome of the two men, and speak with him privately. No more."

"All because he and his friend Tyler rescued you from a would-be rapist on the cross-town shuttle?" That had not been the story she'd first told him.

Jill nodded, unaware of the snare into which she had just fallen. "That is a good reason, I feel." She closed her eyes and wrestled for a time with the blurry, blocked feeling behind her face. A great need for sleep possessed her, which she pushed away. A drug? No.

"I'm sorry I asked, Jill. Forgive me. Of course, your motives were pure."

His voice rang false in her ears, an effect that she dismissed as an illusion born of wine fumes. His image came to her indistinctly and seemed to radiate a nimbus of glowing colors.

"Jill," he asked in a voice deadly serious, "how do you feel about planetary independence?"

"Hm?"

"Freedom from outside interference. Do you favor it strongly? Is it important to you?"

"Course not." She tried to qualify this. "Never gave a damn either way."

"Do you belong to any organizations?"

She frowned, her eyes past seeing. "Course not."

"Do you advocate the expulsion of the Concordat?"

"Don't give damn."

"Whose side are you on?"

"Mine! No one else's—" A last fragment of lucidity came to her, and looking up into the giant face of Richard Temple, her lover, her abductor, her one and only love, she vowed her ultimate manifesto. "I am on my side and no one else's, just as no one is on my side but myself. I am firstly and finally *alone*. The rapist that took me on my seventeenth birthday; my father who cast me out; the women I serve and serve with: These are my enemies. Friends have I none, nor ever shall. Go away and let me sleep."

With a spasm that convulsed her entire body, and yet which she seemed to welcome, she curled up on herself and rolled to the floor.

Richard Temple handled the attentive rush of two nearby waiters with dignity and aplomb. "The lady has had too much to drink. Here is my charge plate; aid me in levering her through the rear door."

A manager and a clerk met them just inside the rear exit.

"A problem, sir?"

"None. The lady is intoxicated. I'll take care of her." A free hand with the wad of large bills that he carried

in his pocket eased the crisis remarkably; two waiters
and the clerk were told to help Temple carry Jill's
unconscious form to the manager's private elevator,
and from there to Temple's ground car. A final flurry
of cash and thanks speeded his departure.

He carried her into his apartment. Less than twelve
hours ago, they had lain in this room and taken their
pleasure on the large double bed in the corner. Each
had misunderstood the other on that occasion; he had
thought her an innocent young woman impulsively
giving herself to a virile and manly officer; she had
taken him to be no more than another man on the
prowl, albeit one from whom classified information
might be illicitly gathered.

He lowered her onto the bed, and quietly stripped
her. She was breathing, in long slow breaths that were
nearly imperceptible, and she was very flushed.

"I seem to have miscalculated the dosage," he muttered; anger took him. In a frenzy he crushed the
remaining carpoules of verificants beneath his heel.
She had made a fool of him, both in public and in the
eyes of his superior; she had evaded him and his questions, and escaped to where he could no longer come at
her. His rage became mixed with other, stronger emotions; he undressed himself, and took his pleasure of
her as if she were no more than an inflatable toy.

The uplands rose swiftly above Camp Epsilon, rich
with the growth of spring. Morning mists hung thick
in the valleys, and above them titanic granite crags
stood watch. Even Tyler was moved, feeling humbled
by the immensity of the scene.

He swung the helicopter around a jagged peak and
swooped low over a tree-clad slope that dropped away
into another mountain valley. Smoke from a cookfire
rose in a vertical column, betraying the presence of a
relatively large settlement. On a second pass he spied
the settlement itself, nestled comfortably between a
broad meadow through which a river meandered, and
the unbroken cliff of solid rock that soared into the sky.

Tyler glanced at Garvey. Garvey shrugged. Nothing was known about this settlement; nothing could be. Tyler indicated his intent to land. Garvey only shrugged again.

Tyler put the helicopter down a good, respectful distance from the village, landing slowly and in a site visible to the doubtlessly suspicious survivors. He had no doubt that several high-powered hunting rifles were already aimed at them as they landed, and more would join them.

The machine settled; the blades slowed and stopped. Garvey started to speak, then stopped and yawned to clear his ears. Ignoring him, Tyler removed the heavy-duty military rifle from the back of the helicopter and assembled the two parts.

"I didn't know you had that along," Garvey stuttered in surprise.

"Right." Tyler's mind was on the job ahead.

"Are you going to let them see it?"

"They already have."

"Hm? How?"

Tyler checked the action on his sidearm and slipped it back into its holster under his jacket. "Binoculars. We're not too far away from that camp."

Garvey digested that in silence.

From here it was less evident than it had been from the air that the camp even existed. The buildings had very likely been built long before the war to serve as a park headquarters or tourist hotel. There was no telling who its current occupants might be.

Tyler climbed out first, his rifle held high above his head as a gesture that he didn't intend to use it unless necessary. Garvey followed him, his hands likewise raised, although he carried no weapons.

The only sounds that they could hear were those of birds and of small animals foraging in the field across the river.

"Uninhabited?" Garvey asked hopefully.

Tyler's eyes flicked to the tall, thin wisp of smoke from some chimney hidden behind the trees. Garvey followed the glance, and shrugged. He'd already known better, but the question had been automatic.

Twenty meters from the edge of the trees, they stopped, waiting there until the people of the forest camp sent out a spokesman. In less than five minutes a voice called out from some indistinguishable point just inside the forest wall.

"What do you want?"

Tyler filled his lungs and bellowed a reply. "We want to parley, meathead! Will you have us wait all day out here?" Garvey stared at him in amazement.

After another short wait, a man emerged from the trees ahead of them and to the left. The newcomer was unarmed, and walked with his arms spread out from his sides. It was clear, however, that his friends were covering him with whatever weapons they had; he was careful never to walk between the camp and the strangers.

The man stopped some five meters from them and regarded them alertly. He was of average height, with short, light-brown hair framing a square, tanned face. Like most men on Theury continent, he bore five weeks' growth of beard, and wore a weary, wary expression. Tyler felt that he had never before seen so many frightened people. He didn't like the effect.

" 'Meathead,' eh? You must be from Saftheur. I recognize the brand of diplomacy. What do you want?"

"No more than information. And I'm not from Saftheur."

" 'Information for information; food's more.' Where *are* you from?"

"Horla continent. I'm with the clean-up crew."

"All right. What do you want to know?"

With a quick motion, Tyler flipped forth the small photo of Potok Empellimin. So fast had he moved that the spokesman from the camp never had a chance to signal the alarm he had felt as Tyler's hand dipped into his jacket. As always, Tyler was taking chances, never fully aware of why he did so.

The spokesman stared dully at the photo for a moment. With a quick glance at Garvey, and back at Tyler, he strode forward and took it from Tyler's hand.

"So?"

"Have you seen him?"

"He a relative of yours?"

"No."

The spokesman shrugged. "No secret. I've not seen him, and that's 'cause he's not been through here. No one's been." He thought for a moment. "Horla continent is putting together some big rescue effort?"

"Not too big, but it'll be enough. About halfway between here and the wreck of Vis city is a base camp. Do you have a radio and a radioman?"

The spokesman nodded.

"Good," Tyler continued. "Have him tune it to 1.12 megahertz, and you'll get some news. You can reply at 1.07."

The spokesman for the camp said nothing. Considering that Tyler had failed to get the information he had been seeking, Garvey was anxious to leave. Tyler was in no hurry, however, and Garvey reminded himself of his promised reward, forcing himself to remain patient. In sudden panic he looked over his shoulder, afraid that some of the survivors might have maneuvered in such a way as to cut Tyler and him off from the helicopter. No one was in sight, but the fright stayed with him. In this area, in the world that had come into being since the war, any lack of caution could be fatal.

"Other settlements about here?" Tyler was asking.

"From the air, you'll be able to follow the highway up into the mountains. The bridges are all down, but that won't bother you. The road forks some fifty kilometers north of here, and you'll probably head west . . ."

Tyler stood at apparent ease, his rifle leaning against his side as if forgotten. Garvey felt his own lack of armament keenly, although he was able to see distinctly that the spokesman for the camp was likewise unarmed.

"Bandits?"

"We've run off a few."

"How were they armed?"

"Small arms, hunting rifles. Nothing to speak of. We have some scouts out, and this terrain makes ambushes real easy."

The distinction between bandit and survivor was blurred, Garvey knew. The kindest man alive can become a hellishly cruel savage when his entire civilization crumbles overnight. Again and again Garvey's back itched with his knowledge of the guns that must be trained upon him. And their helicopter was an inducement to banditry that would be very hard to ignore. Even with no refueling possible, it would increase this valley settlement's survival chances nearly a hundredfold.

With a chill, Garvey spied a figure off to his left, near the riverbank, creeping up behind an almost adequate screen of high weeds. He got only a glimpse before the figure blended back into his cover, but it was clear that the person had been closing in. Was it simply insurance? Were they doing no more than taking reasonable precautions? *Please, Tyler, get us out of here.* The Concordat agent seemed in no great hurry to leave. He was swapping information for information, guardedly piecing together an overall picture of life in the hinterland, while giving away no more than he needed to. Was he totally oblivious to the ambush that was shaping up?

Glancing at his wristwatch, Tyler nodded abstractedly at what the spokesman had just said, and jerked a thumb over his shoulder toward the helicopter. "We'd best be moving on, then."

"Why?" asked the spokesman, his eyes betraying no guilt. "Things were just getting profitable. And I'd like to know when the rescue effort will be getting back up here into the hills."

Garvey caught another glimpse, this time of two more figures sneaking along the water's edge.

"I have no doubt that they'll get here eventually," Tyler said evenly.

"But only after they've helped the lowlands."

Tyler gave him an inquisitive look.

"That's always been the way of it," the spokesman explained. "The lowlands get the best of everything, and the back-country has to pay for it."

"Isn't that an argument for a more central government, then?"

As the spokesman allowed that it might be, while retaining some cynical doubt, Garvey almost gasped as his impatience to be away and free caught at his breath. He felt suffocated here on the ground, when inside a minute he and Tyler could be aloft, safe, untrapped.

Tyler broke into the spokesman's naive discourse with a hurried, "We've got to go. Now. Garvey, come."

Garvey was more than happy to, and only with difficulty restrained himself from running ahead. It was to his immense surprise when Tyler burst into a flat-out run toward the helicopter, dodging first this way, then the other. With an oath, Garvey followed suit, dashing hurriedly upon Tyler's heels.

Tyler threw himself into the cockpit and kicked in the full power starter. As the rotor blades jerked into motion, Garvey scrambled in. The blades blurred into full motion and the vehicle lifted with a lurch. Below him, Garvey could see the complete outlines of the ambush that had been about to close upon them. Five men and women were strung out along the river, small-bore rifles at their sides, watching their quarry soar to freedom. Tyler nudged Garvey's arm and pointed to the cliff-face, where three more individuals clung, weapons slung over their shoulders.

The roar of the blades made conversation impossible, and when he saw the feral grin on James Tyler's face, Garvey wasn't sorry for this. Tyler had known about the intended ambush, yet hadn't warned his partner nor hurried his business.

That night, as they camped on a steep-sloping upland meadow under a sky resplendent with all the countless stars that a rare cloudless night could reveal, Tyler broached the subject.

"I needed to know," he said, in a voice so low that Garvey needed to strain to hear despite the chill night's calm. "I needed to know just how badly civilization has been buried in the minds of the survivors. It's been just over five weeks since the bombs fell, and already the high civilization of your dominant culture is dead and forgotten."

Garvey wanted to dispute this, but felt himself too unsure of Tyler's mood to chance it.

"This entire continent is without art, without joy. No civilization remains. They would have waylaid us for our food and guns, let alone the helicopter."

His words trailed off, and Garvey, assuming the subject to be closed, drifted off to restful sleep. Tyler mused darkly as he lay in his own sleeping bag on the thick grassy slope under the infinite sky.

Civilization is so fragile. A well-tuned economy can become ill-conditioned so easily; a period of artistic quiescence can lead to a puritan ethos. Religious fervor is only with difficulty channeled away from its natural path of destruction. We buried the gods long ago, but gods, like treasures, don't sleep peacefully in their graves.

Our technology is the strongest thing we have. It keeps our cities lit at night; it binds us together; it feeds us. But if a single aspect of our technology was denied us, we would collapse. Could a city function without electricity? Could our farms produce the high yield they do without chemical aid?

This continent has been denied all of its technical resources by the war that they brought upon themselves. How long will it take us to rebuild them?

Who would there be to rebuild us?

Dawn arrived with a thick, dripping fog that clung to the entire mountainside. The stillness was nearly tangible, and faraway noises seemed eerily close. While Garvey yet slept, Tyler roused himself, to make his way quietly down the slope to a mountain stream that rushed icily under the trees below the meadow. Putting his heavy rifle aside, he bent to drink.

He was momentarily helpless, as the dacelot chose that time to attack.

The sleek form burst from heavy undergrowth to Tyler's left, darting toward what it sensed to be helpless prey. Tyler looked up from the stream, saw it, and shot it with the pistol he had unconsciously drawn. Hit hard in breast and flank, the beast completed its leap without volition. A sandy-colored blur of fur and muscle, it landed heavily upon Tyler, its killer, who was scrambling awkwardly halfway into the creek. Hissing through distended jaws, the beast stiffened, swiping viciously at the soft mud of the creekbank, and died, drowning in its own blood.

By the time Garvey arrived, roused by the gunshots, Tyler was sitting and shivering on the far side of the stream, completely drenched with coldest snow-melt.

Garvey took in the scene quickly. Without a further glance at the dead hunting beast, he pulled off his jacket and tossed it to Tyler, who caught and donned it gratefully. Garvey returned his attention to the animal.

"A dacelot. And starved half to death."

"Five weeks since the war," Tyler stuttered, wracked with shivering from his icy immersion, "and the human survivors have depleted all the wild game."

"We have to eat something," Garvey said reasonably. He prodded the corpse of the pouncer. Tyler watched disinterestedly. The off-white pelt of the beast was unlovely in death, even where its blood was not smeared. The matted fur and tattered ears, fibrils, and snub tail gave mute evidence of how desperate the animal's plight had become, until starvation had forced its attack on unfamiliar prey.

How long has it been since I last killed? Tyler wondered as he looked over the wrecked hunting-beast. Hunched within his dripping jackets, he let his mind veer into the past. *The last man I shot was at Down-Norton spaceport on—Petalmo? He had just seen me, and drawn his own weapon. Then . . .* He now sat and remembered without pride the precision of the shot and the heady rush of strong emotional fulfillment

that he had felt that day. At the official inquiry he
had been obnoxious, as only he could be. When finally
released, he had been incredibly snide, reloading his
pistol ostentatiously as a not-so-subtle reminder that
no law could touch him, who was a law unto himself.

The corpse of the dacelot had ceased oozing blood
and lay motionless, its powerful hindquarters dragging in the stream. Garvey stood by it, watching Tyler
anxiously.

"Go up to the helicopter," Tyler said, forcing the
words through jaws that chattered from the cold, "and
get the firestarter. I'll wait here."

Garvey nodded, glad to be doing something. In a
moment he was gone, trudging up the hill and through
the trees.

Alone with the dead dacelot and the gurgling stream,
Tyler fought to control his thoughts. He tried to dis-
miss his turmoil as a result of the chill and the closeness of the brief combat. Despite this, his emotions
spun quietly about him, leaving him unmoved at their
center. He remembered, almost with shame, the fight
he had picked with Commander Denis of the recovery
mission, back in the prefabricated town that was Emergency city. He remembered with a pang the row he
had caused back at Camp Epsilon.

And in the corpse of the dacelot he saw the face of
the first person he'd ever killed, a young woman whom
he had been led to, set up with, and betrayed by, all on
one windy night on the world of his birth. It had been
a conspiracy, and it had backfired, leading to the woman's death and the imprisonment of Tyler and several
others. If originally he was to have been the one to die,
to have been the principal victim of the ill-conceived
trap, he nevertheless had suffered heavily for the act.

Why was this coming to his mind now? He thrust
the thoughts from him, hoping for them never to re-
surface. He hadn't thought about her for years, knowing that the pain of her betrayal had scarred him
deeply. Her face seemed familiar—as if, perhaps, he'd
recently met someone who in some way resembled her.
He forced his mind on towards more productive avenues.

I'm a killer. Today proves that. The Concordat recruiter who found me pacing my confinement in First Prison back home saw immediately what I was. From the moment I enlisted with the Navy, I was predestined to be a part of their operation Black Book; from the first, all they wanted was a killer. I guess I've satisfied them.

Garvey returned then, with a silent power saw, the firestarter, and a blanket. While Tyler shucked his sopping clothes, Garvey sliced up a small pile of dead branches and played the firestarter over it. The dry wood crumpled noisily into a white-glowing mound of coals and blazing twigs. Tyler moved greedily closer.

Across from the fire, Garvey sat cross-legged, toying with the power saw. He waved it negligently at small chips of wood left over from his earlier tree-trimming. Along the invisible line of force projected from the small, stubby cylinder, the wood flakes glowed and parted. The effect was limited to a distance of just under one meter from the projector. The severed edges of the wood were shiny, hard, and cool to the touch. Garvey speculatively eyed one of the tall trees that grew nearby, crowding the stream's bank.

"Don't try it," Tyler said, while holding his jacket first one way, then the other toward the fire to dry it.

"Would it work?" Garvey asked, slightly awed.

"Yeah, but that'd wear out the power cell too fast."

Respectfully setting the device aside, Garvey glanced at the firestarter, then at Tyler's three guns. "Don't you have anything along that isn't also a weapon?"

"No, not really." His eyes challenged Garvey, who spread his hands peaceably, while in no wise deferring.

After a time, Garvey set off again up-slope to check on their camp, and to bring back something in the way of provisions. Tyler strolled back down to the creek-bank and looked over the corpse of the dacelot. Finally, he grabbed it by a forepaw and dragged it away downstream, out of sight.

Over coffee and hard biscuits, Garvey finally brought up the subject he'd been most intrigued by since the attempted ambush in the valley. "Who is the man in the photograph?"

Tyler took it in stride. "Someone I'm searching for."

"Don't tell me, if you don't want to." Garvey waited a tactful moment and let slip, "It's plain you mean to kill him."

Tyler turned him a sour glance, and called upon the acting talent that some people sensed in him. "He was the Concordat representative and coordinator, living in Vis city. While conducting interviews down in Emergency city, we found a guy who saw him up in these hills. The part about my investigating the idea of taking this world fully into the Concordat is also true, as it happens. But since I was getting nowhere in that pursuit, they told me to try and chase down our lost ambassador."

Garvey digested this for a few moments, finally to smile quietly into the campfire. It was plain that he didn't believe a word of it. Tyler turned his gaze elsewhere.

By late morning they had gathered up their gear and climbed the hill up to the helicopter. They crawled in, Tyler kicking over the engine and throwing the machine into the sky with a gut-wrenching swiftness.

For the most part, he navigated by stream beds and valleys, veering away from them occasionally when an old roadway crossed on bridges that sometimes hung intact, and sometimes were crumbled down into the streams. Along these highways the wrecks of cars could be seen, their engines stilled for lack of fuel. No people were in sight.

Most of that day they circled, weaving a chain-net over the mountains. Only once before four o'clock did they spy a human being, and he was partially sheltered behind a fallen tree, evidently terrified of the approaching helicopter. Tyler passed him by without further molestation.

Partway up a wooded slope was a great blackened patch where a fire had raged unchecked. Passing low over it, the two searchers could see the wreck of a

small airplane near its lower verge. Only the wetness
of the spring season had kept the fire from engulfing
the entire forest for kilometers about. Tyler reflected
upon the irony with a sick, sour whimsy, leaving the
site of the crash far behind. *Always declare nuclear
war in early spring. Fires won't spread, and there's still
time for the survivors to reinvent stone-age agriculture.
In all mythologies preserved by cultures evolved from
hunting-gathering primitives, the spring season is a
time of renewal and rebirth. What a fitting time to
vaporize a few billion people.*

While he thought about the irony of despair and
hope, his eyes darted over the tree-clad slopes below
him. Once a flock of heavy birds rose in alarm from
their feast, frightened away by the heavy chopping
roar of the helicopter. Tyler had no desire to see what
they had been eating. In a nearly inaccessible valley
headed by a thundering waterfall, a fat herd of graz-
ing beasts sheltered, living happily on the lush green
growth along the water's edge. If they were found by
survivors, their dried meat could mean the difference
between civilization and savagery, pushing back the
need for cannibalism until the hastily and improperly
planted crops could grow to harvest-ripeness.

Mythology again seized Tyler's thoughts. *Agricul-
tural societies sometimes develop monotheism, and the
form that is most common is the figure of the great,
patient harvester, who cuts down men in their prime,
judging and separating the worthy from the spoiled.*

His instincts rebelled against this type of analysis.
His business was well-defined; this philosophizing only
emphasized the brutality of his profession.

A nudge from Garvey recalled him from his reverie.
The guide pointed downward, indicating that he wished
Tyler to land. Tyler shrugged and began to comply,
taking the machine through a sweeping half-turn
toward a clear spot.

"What's up, Garvey?" he asked, once the rotors had
stopped.

"About a mile back, I saw a file of men and women,

all armed, moving along an upland trail." He worked his jaws to clear his altitude-plugged ears. "It looked like an organized attack."

Tyler blinked. Had he been deep enough in thought to have missed that? He pulled a map from its case under the pilot's seat, and pushed it into Garvey's hands, pointing at it. "We're here. Where were they?"

"On this ridge, heading north. They all had rifles. When we flew past they took cover, but I could see them anyway."

Tyler studied the map, looking for the probable target of the stealthy attack. It was quickly evident that they had been heading for a small town named Marano, nestled high in a small valley up against the mountain wall. If Garvey was right in his location of the column of bandits, this town was due for an onslaught soon, probably tomorrow at sunrise.

"How many were there?"

"I saw at least twenty, and I'm pretty sure there were more."

Tyler thought this over. With his heavy combat rifle, he could easily stand off any ten people armed with no more than hunting rifles. Alternatively, using the helicopter as a hovering gun platform, he could block the advance, keep them from moving farther uphill. For the third time that day Tyler felt a shade of the infinite power that a single, universal god might feel as it stood above a cringing primitive to topple the savage with a power as pure as wrath.

And that's why a thinking man is better than any omnipotent monodeity, he thought as he churned the helicopter's engine back into surging life. *I can only guess at what is right. That means I have to try to take all the factors into consideration before I act. Simply to swoop down upon that column of would-be soldiers would be the crude act of a man obsessed with his tactical advantage.*

He threw in the clutch and felt the machine lift under him. Following a circuitous route, knowing all the time that he was choosing his decision freely, he headed over the titanic, tilted landscape toward the small town.

Just before sunset they arrived over the junction of three roads that marked the site of the town of Marano. The bridges over all three approaches were down; white water foamed over the crumbled concrete blocks that lay at the bottom of their chasms. The town had no more than forty roofs, including a large public meeting hall, several stores, shops, and stables. Not far away stood a ranching and farming complex, its block barns and warehouses gaily painted and shining under the lengthening rays of the setting sun.

No people were visible, but the town looked well-tended and clean. No smoke rose from any of the town's several chimneys, but laundry was hung on lines in backyards, and herd animals, lean yet healthy, milled about in pens. Tyler's trained eye picked out a dozen spots where lightly armed men could very well be hiding, waiting for the machine invader to land so that its occupants might be killed.

Every pane of glass was in place and intact; the street was swept. These indications convinced Tyler that at least one of his fears was false: that the column of "invaders" had been the original citizens of this town planning to recover it by force from marauding conquerors. He set the helicopter down smoothly in the exact center of town, where the three roads joined in a T-shaped intersection.

From this angle the town looked menacingly close. The nearest building was no more than twelve meters away; there was enough cover for a hundred ambushers.

Tyler started to climb from the machine. Garvey grabbed his shoulder.

"Don't go."

Without taking his eyes off the scene before him, Tyler said in a low voice, "It'll be all right. Stay here, if you want."

"Wouldn't that look bad? Like I was covering you?"

"We'd both be safer if you came along, that's true."

"All right, then," Garvey said, breathing deeply. He

released his harness and stepped out at the same time as Tyler. Just as before, Tyler carried along his large combat rifle, holding it well away from his body in his left hand. His two pistols were concealed, but Garvey knew with what swiftness they could spring into his hands. With no choice, Garvey left his fate with Tyler, and tried to feel the trust that he must display.

After a few minutes they ended up side by side near an apparently abandoned supplies and feed store. The sun was setting behind them, casting their shadows sharply onto the sliding door of the feed-barn. Garvey could only assume they were completely alone in a town deserted for a reason he couldn't guess.

Tyler labored under no such false assumptions. He not only expected the voice that spoke next, but anticipated it by turning gently toward it before it had begun.

"What are you two doing here?"

Tyler could see nothing in the glare of the setting sun; the ambush had moved between it and him. He kept his eyes open, although the light stung them, and held his body motionless. Garvey, next to him, gasped and whirled, then froze.

"Come on out where I can see you," Tyler said reasonably.

"Throw aside your gun."

With a casualness that impressed Garvey, Tyler did so, flinging the rifle into the deepening shadows with brutal force. His hunting pistol followed it, but not his fighting pistol. The sun was now down, fully out of sight behind the lesser mountain range across the great valley below the town. Tyler's eyes, light-struck, began slowly to adjust to the deep twilight.

A figure detached itself from the shadows in front of them. Easing forward, it approached the two searchers, striding forward menacingly. Garvey's stomach seemed to knot up with his fear, but he made no display. Tyler waited, completely at ease.

Finally, as the man stepped near, Tyler and Garvey could see him. He was of late middle age, tall and slim, yet imposing, his hair speckled with gray. He wore his hair short, and was clean-shaven. His hands were gnarled, his face tanned. And his expression was menacing. He looked into Garvey's face, searching for something, something that he didn't seem to find. Next he bent his face toward Tyler's, and gazed long at him, his pale blue eyes looking closely into Tyler's cold gray ones.

The townsman's challenge, implicit in his aggressive gaze, went unanswered by Tyler who, either from respect or from caution, kept his expression neutral. Nevertheless, Garvey, watching sharply, saw the power and strength that Tyler kept in check, and saw that the townsman could feel it, too.

Before the situation could grow dangerously uncomfortable, Garvey interposed, saying in a voice deliberately thin and nervous, "It's getting dark. Could we have some light?"

The townsman swung toward him, giving him a looking-over that was somehow like a physical beating. Then, turning away, the man called aloud, "Jacob! Rolf! Turn the lights on!"

And with a clang, floodlights on tall poles slammed on, lighting the town, but more importantly lighting the town's perimeter so that anyone trying to sneak close would be harshly revealed. Under their glare, the townsman was diminished slightly, seeming now no more than a hardened farmer, rough and rude in contrast to his slightly more civilized guests. Garvey felt acutely conscious of his five-week beard, however, when the townsman, Tyler, and the two tall men who now approached were all clean-shaven.

"What do you want here?" the townsman rasped, flanked now by the two newcomers.

"Two things," Tyler said smoothly, his air of easy assurance masking the tautness of his belly muscles, the nerves of his right arm that sang with readiness. He was acutely aware of the bulk that his fighting pistol made, heavy and reassuring under his arm. "Did you know that there's a column of people climbing up the valley, all of them armed?"

"Damn, Loyd, I told you they'd be back."

"Quiet, Jacob. Remember, I agreed with you." The townsman turned back to Tyler, who was carefully gauging his reaction and the reactions of his two friends. "Where did you see them, and how many were there?"

"Garvey, show them the map." Tyler noted with a trace of amusement that although Loyd and Jacob squatted with Garvey and himself to study the map that was spread on the yet-warm pavement, the youngest of the three townsmen stood back, watching alertly, his rifle barrel never leaving its direct aim at Tyler's head.

"Crack-Brady canyon," snarled Jacob. Tyler and Loyd turned to look at him. A tall, broad-shouldered, thin-faced man with an unruly tousle of deep-brown hair, Jacob seemed the personification of resentment and revenge; cold anger seeped from him. Tyler was able to recognize the killer in him, and the sort of personality that would gladly die if he were only able to send an enemy to hell ahead of him. "They've got a local boy or two with them, to know that canyon."

"Maybe they've just got a map, like this one."

"Nope. The maps don't show it clearly enough, how the brush grows so thick up there, and the trees come right down to the old dam."

Tyler found the dam on the map without difficulty. Well below the town, it represented no threat if blown or burst, and little in the way of needed water resource. The town would be just as well off without it, drawing water from deep wells. But it wasn't the dam itself that concerned these men, Tyler discovered, looking more closely at the map. From the dam, a clear avenue of attack into the town existed, along a high ridge of rock that climbed gently upward until it crested just below the road junction. It would be hard to defend, and would lend the advantage to the side with even a slight numerical superiority.

"When we flew over this spot," Garvey said, "I saw about twenty of them, men and women, all armed. I'm sure there were more."

"Women!" Jacob spat. Tyler thought of the Concordat's 44th Marine Division, whose complement was about one-third women. What would this Jacob think of being sent sprawling by a large, angry woman with scientific martial arts skill? The Concordat surrounded them all, and was so far away. On this world, women were little better than herd animals, plummeted from their prewar status. The force that was intent on taking over this town was plainly desperate, to use their second-class citizens in the assault force.

"You said *two* things," Loyd reminded. "What's the other?"

Under the sharp eyes of the young man with the rifle, Tyler drew out the photograph. "I'm looking for this man. I think he's been through this area."

Jacob moved to look at it, but Loyd held it close to himself. "Why do you want him?"

"He was the Concordat representative to Vistheur. I'm here to try to rescue him." He felt Garvey stir at his side, but neither of them had any reason to say more at this time. Tyler could trust Garvey, or he was no judge of character.

Mention of the Concordat had an unpleasant effect upon the three men. Loyd became grim; Jacob grimaced, turned his head, and spat; the youth with the rifle made a great production of levering a shell into the chamber. The night began to feel very cold.

"Are you from the damned star-tyrants?" Loyd asked gently.

"Yes," Tyler said simply. "I am."

"Well, then, you can—"

"Wait a minute," snapped Garvey. "I'm Vis, and I can prove it. This guy's all right. Down south, they're putting together a big relief effort, in order to save everybody they can from starving this winter. He's promised my camp a self-contained fusion generator, which will make the difference between life and death for up to three hundred people."

"We've already got one," Jacob said icily.

"It's buried five chains deep, out beneath father's

farm," the young man with the rifle said, a trace of pride in his voice. Tyler had noticed the floodlights, and surmised as much.

"Rescue effort, eh? How big?" Loyd prepared himself to listen to what he considered a load of star-tyrant guff. At the same time, he took another close look at the photograph.

"The whole continent is dead," Tyler said quietly, trying to avoid the tone of a lecturer or a pamphleteer. "Our satellites in orbit . . ." He saw Loyd bridle. "By treaty, everything above two hundred kilometers is ours."

"They never asked me," Loyd snapped. "Get on with your story."

"We saw over fifteen hundred warheads impact. We couldn't stop it, but we came in afterward to try to feed the starving, heal the burned, cure the sick."

"And take over our world. Well, to hell with that. That farm"—he flung his arm over his shoulder to indicate the spread—"is mine. And when I die, it goes to my son. We don't need any star-tyrant interference." Loyd frowned. "I'm sorry that the cities died. Sorrier than you might know. But now that they're gone, we don't need new ones."

"What do you raise on that farm?" Tyler asked in a reasonable tone.

"Livestock and grains. What's it to you?"

"How many people did you once feed?"

"I guess I don't know. But I can feed this town, and maybe a little bit more. My son's sons will eventually clear this whole valley, and maybe build a wall to keep the cutthroats out. Vistheur is dead, but so are their tax collectors."

A feudalism in the making, Tyler thought. *Within five generations, unchecked, they'll have evolved a full nobility-landholder aristocracy.*

By this time it had grown quite dark, so that the harsh glare of the floodlights cast multiple sharp shadows over the rough pavement of the old road. The chill of the mountain night crept up from the valleys; countless stars glittered in the black heavens.

Loyd glanced up at the arrival of a pair of young men with rifles. "Is everything under control, boss?"

"Get back to where I posted you!" Loyd snapped.

The men hurried away.

"Come on, then. Let's get in out of the cold." Accepting his rough invitation, Tyler and Garvey followed him down the highway and through a gate. Jacob and the youth came along three paces behind, maintaining watchfulness.

As they passed through the gate, the two outsiders were met by a titanic black watchbeast. It leaped to its feet and strained at its chain, roaring balefully at these people it did not recognize. Garvey flinched back. Tyler's hand flew to his jacket, but instead of drawing his pistol, he turned the motion into a feint that covered for the savage kick he dealt the creature where its forelegs joined its body. Without pausing, he whipped his linked hands down onto the beast's arching neck. The beast backed away, its roars muted but unceasing, while Tyler stood with exaggerated stillness under the muzzle of the rifle that the young man pushed aggressively at him.

Loyd said only, "I'm glad someone finally did that." He motioned for Tyler and Garvey to enter the house that was before them. Vine-covered, of stone and shiplapped wood, the house stood back from the street, its windows lit yet curtained.

The young man carefully set the rifle aside, leaning it against the wall of the building just under a small porch-roof, leaving him no weapon to cover his prisoners. It was done so automatically that Tyler for the first time appreciated what primitive, harsh discipline the youth must have been raised under, so that the rules of the house came unthinkingly before common sense. Obedience was built into him with as much precision as if it had been machined into his frame by electroengraving.

The interior of the room was quaint by Tyler's tastes. Although evidently a living room that served also as a reception and dining room, it was cramped, the ancient furniture placed in ancestrally ordained sites, regardless of through-traffic flow. Because of this, one corner of the large, hand-wrought rug that partially covered the floor was frayed into nonexistence through overuse, while its far corner was untouched, unfaded. Sun-bleached photographs of a pair of forebears hung on the wall, warped by the heat that gusted from an open-hearth fireplace. From inside, he could see the clever arrangement that took the smoke from the large fire and bubbled it through a home-built water filter, so that no smoke rose over the horizon to betray the town.

Garvey saw the room as falling within a specific cultural context, and pangs of nostalgia swept through him. In such a home his grandmother had lived, across the continent and high in a different range of mountains. The smells of fresh and of stale cooking, of the house-thest in its cage by the window, and of the people themselves awoke warm, loving memories in him. The question about what Tyler might do next concerned him, although so far his behavior had been proper.

Tyler took in the room, the decoration, the scents, with a minimum of unease. Viewed in their own context, the surroundings would be designed to give comfort and security. The relative smallness of the room indicated a greater need for close human contact than he would have felt; the temperature was kept at a constant, close-in, baking warmth.

Loyd was greeted in the middle of the room by a pair of women, one elderly, one in early middle age. They looked at Tyler and Garvey with a pronounced, studied, exact neutrality, glancing from the two strangers to Loyd, and then back. By degrees, as they absorbed his subliminally expressed antagonism, they adopted this view, until within less than a minute, they were nearly glaring their hatred, although Loyd had never spoken. Tyler was inwardly amused by this plastic form of response, knowing that if Loyd had been smiling even in the slightest, the two women would have been equally effusive in their welcome. Did either have a personality in her own right?

Garvey glanced at Tyler, and then stepped in with the correct introductions. "Ladies. I'm Fulmer Garvey, and this is James Tyler."

They grinned, strainedly, and backed away a trifle.

Loyd took over. "I'm Loyd Shayler; this is my brother Jacob, and my son Rolf. This is Emma Tilgen, and her mother, Willa Tilgen. Let's sit down." It was an order, although Tyler saw that Loyd himself didn't know it.

"Where are you from, Mr. Tyler?" Emma asked, a question that she seemed comfortable with, to be asked of any guest as a way of opening conversation.

"Mr. Tyler's a star-tyrant," Loyd said maliciously, as much to shock the women as to discomfort Tyler. Sensing a challenge, the word-fighter in Tyler began to flex its limbs.

"Actually, I'm a Navy man, myself, with the reserve fleet that's orbiting overhead right now."

"Warships, most likely," Jacob snarled. Tyler sensed a weak spot and lied in order to exploit it.

"Yes. About a hundred, some of them quite large." Actually, the fleet with which he had arrived numbered less than twenty Scouts and Destroyers, eighteen transports, albeit one a troop carrier, and a hospital ship.

"And what are they here for?" Jacob said, drawing breath to angrily answer his own rhetorical question.

Garvey, more quickly, put in. "To try to help the starving survivors of our war."

Good for you, Garvey, thought Tyler. "We've got transports full of fresh food, clean water, high-technology medicines. We're helping in every way we can." His matter-of-fact tone took the fight from Jacob, who only muttered.

"What will it cost us?" Loyd asked shrewdly.

"What did you pay in taxes last year?" Tyler retorted. "You can bet that we'll ask less. *We* don't have anything we need to prove."

"What do you mean by that?" challenged Loyd.

"What did the government of Vistheur spend that

money on? Nuclear missiles. Well, those are all gone.
The Concordat is above such stupidity."

Loyd's outburst in response to that so startled Tyler
that he almost went for his gun. "Don't ever speak
that way again," he roared, "or I'll send you dancing
with a whip!"

"Now, Loyd," murmured Emma, lightly urging the
older man to resume his seat.

"He lost his wife in the war," Emma tried to whisper. "She was in Vis city—"

"I'll give my own explanations, woman," Loyd rasped.
Emma subsided.

"That's the way of it," Loyd continued, his face red.
"Don't use words of war in my house." The momentary
glance that Emma gave Loyd suggested to Tyler that
the house might not be as much the old farmer's as he
might suppose; without comment, Emma again took
up the silent role of loyal supporter.

"I won't apologize," Tyler said, regaining some of his
lost enthusiasm. "Ever since I arrived here, I've been
maligned, railed against, and denounced. 'Star-tyrant'
you call me. I'll say only that the Concordat is no gang
of tyrants, and you'd be well advised to try to understand them before you condemn them."

"Are you here to take us over, or aren't you?" Loyd
asked without much heat.

"I'll be honest. We don't know yet."

Jacob whooped and brought his fist down on the
table. Emma and Willa looked uncomfortable, and Rolf
looked completely bewildered. Loyd sat unmoving.

"I say we shoot him and take his helicopter," Jacob
sputtered, moving as if to stand.

"Be still, Jacob!" Loyd said, and that was enough.

King of the mountain, Tyler mused. *He's got no reason to want civilization to be restored.* Aloud: "How
many bandits do you run off each week? Will it get
better or worse?" His voice dropped slightly. "And
what will you do when you run out of bullets?" He let
that sink in. "We can't avoid talk of war; you've got a
war going right now. The bandits are getting orga-

nized because they have to. How big an army can you hold off?"

"We've run 'em off before, and we'll do it again tomorrow."

"How many of your people die each time through?"

Pain disfigured Loyd's face for a moment.

"We can do it as long as we have to," Jacob tossed in. "They're starving; we're not."

"What if we were to feed them, and control them at the same time? What's wrong with that?"

"Because you'd want to control us, too." Loyd sighed. "I've seen it before. Taxes go up, but we get less. The only government I'm loyal to is self-government."

"What if you were to give food to the bandits so that they'd leave you alone?" Tyler asked, intending to draw the analogy between that and voluntary taxation. It was the wrong tack.

"Hell no!" Loyd's patience was nearing its end. "They'd just want more next time, and we'd be giving them the strength to attack us at the end."

"I beg leave to withdraw the subject." Tyler's face was pale. It occurred to him finally that these people had made up their minds, and that the dividing line between logical argument and mortal insult was vanishingly slim. There could be no debate with minds as set in their ways as these.

Nevertheless . . .

"Hell no. You brought it up; you live with it. We want to be let alone, and we've got that right. Understand?"

"Maybe not." Tyler said this with a sincere gentleness that took Garvey by surprise. Inwardly, the latter cringed, awaiting Tyler's eventual anger . . . or worse.

But it had at last penetrated Tyler's mind that his cover occupation—investigating the viability of the world's neutrality—extended upward as well as downward. He would actually be called upon to write a report and make a recommendation. The idea of responsibility took him unprepared, and he found that he didn't like the bound feeling it gave him.

"What would you be doing right now if your farm had burned to the ground, and this village also, in a wildfire started by the ..."

Jacob glared, but Loyd gave the question some thought. "I'd hitch up a draybeast and start plowing."

"How long would it take you to begin to feed this village on the crops you'd raise?"

"Month, month and a half ... we've got the livestock to last that long."

"No. They died in the fire, or escaped."

"We'd hunt."

"The bandits are hunting."

"Yeah, well, we'd just divide up the range with the bandits. They can go downhill, and we'll hunt up here. What's ..."

"There are more people downhill than the range can feed. You know that. How many wild, edible herbivores are you going to find per square kilometer? But that's not the point. How far to the next town with a good collection of livestock?"

Rolf answered, the first words he'd said since entering. "About six miles up Jumlee creek—the Olive ranch."

Loyd nodded. Tyler continued. "And here you are starving, being harried by the bandits ... Do you see what I'm driving at?"

"Old man Olive would take us in; we're oldest of friends." Despite this assurance, Loyd looked uneasy. He'd reasoned it through, further, perhaps, than he could have wished to.

"Just like we took in the Hendersons from down Thyck canyon," Emma put in, not at all aware of Tyler's train of logic.

"The Hendersons are out on the line, right now, aren't they?" Tyler asked. "On scout duty?"

"Damn!" Loyd cursed, taking the forgotten duty as an excuse to cut off the debate. "Rolf, Jacob, we ought to get down to the outpost and tell them about the bandits."

"I don't see why," mumbled Jacob. "They know they're in the area."

"Jacob, you fool; they don't know about the bandits coming up Crack-Brady canyon."

"What?" fluttered Emma. Willa looked as if she wanted to shrink out of sight.

"Now, Emma, it's nothing more than another load of ruffians, like last time."

"Last time, four boys died," Emma said, torn between defiance and submission.

Loyd eyed Tyler. The knowledge of eventual defeat was upon him, defeat not to the bandits, but to the larger and slower evil of government, taxation, and the endless combat with the market that occupies the time and effort of any farmer.

"They can't get here until morning, and there aren't that many of them," he said to Emma with unpracticed tenderness. "We'll turn them back."

"Don't you get killed, Loyd Shayler." Loyd made no response as he ushered Tyler and Garvey out the door. Rolf grabbed his rifle, and a dim understanding came to him of how his charges had been inside the house without any protection for Emma and Willa. He shrugged it off. Loyd and Jacob, between them, could no doubt subdue and hogtie any two flatland strangers. No one made any comment when, as they walked down the road, Tyler made a detour to pick up his hunting pistol and heavy combat rifle, or when Garvey strayed by the grounded helicopter to get a compact radio transceiver.

A kilometer farther on, Rolf got up the nerve to ask about the weaponry. "What kind of rifle's that, Mr. Tyler?"

"Marines issue, heavy weapons Guard Company accelerator rifle. Effective range of over eight hundred meters."

"Gods!"

Walking through the darkness, now beyond the range of the floodlights, they had sorted themselves out into a file, and upon leaving the main road had found a well-worn dirt trail leading down one of the many canyons into the gulleys below. Some stars were visible, but a very light haze blotted out all but the brightest. It was too late in the evening for the specks of light that were the small detachment of spaceships to be visible as they orbited overhead, but Tyler noticed Rolf looking anyhow.

Loyd broke the silence some minutes later. "Will I be allowed to keep my farm if . . . the Concordat takes over?"

Tyler heard the effort in Loyd's voice as he avoided saying "star-tyrants." "I think so. There's more good land than there are people to work it. All it means—"

"I know what it means." *All I wanted was for my son to be all he could be,* Loyd thought, as they marched through the tall weeds to either side of the trail. *He could have married little Tracy Olive and been owner of both ranches. His children would have grown up free of fear, because he'd have finished what I started, clearing all these hills of bandits.*

Tyler's mind was running along a different yet parallel path. *He doesn't think of the bandits as people. Why should he? Damn it, I'm not here to fight his fight for him, nor, really, to help reestablish civilization on this continent. I'm here to kill a man. I don't know what court, if any, sentenced him to die, but if he's as guilty as it looks of starting this war, then he deserves death. I'm the one to see that he gets it.*

As for tomorrow's firefight, I know whose side I'm on.

"Look, Mr. Tyler," Loyd forced out after another long silence, "I don't mind cooperating with a few of my neighbors, and as long as there's a market, I'll sell my produce at a fair price. But why in fire do we need a real government? Why does the Concordat need to step in and take over everything?"

"Because . . ." Tyler began, and began again with surprising gentleness, "because there's almost nothing left to take over." He walked in silence for a time. "The cities are gone. The factories are gone. Almost eight billion people are gone. Not because there was too much government, but because there was too little.

Because people wouldn't accept a world government, let alone unification with the Concordat, petty rivalries led to absolute waste of this entire continent.

"And that's why the Concordat exists: not to rule, not to dictate, but to coordinate, so as to minimize duplication of effort, and reduce waste. The taxes you'd pay us would be less than you've ever paid before."

"Big talk," Loyd finally retorted. "Tomorrow the bandits attack, and how many boys will I lose in the sniping? Your almighty Concordat is too far away to help me. I'm entirely dependent on my men, who I can trust to shoot straight, by my orders."

Tyler held his peace, until he could persuade himself to let the matter drop. Part of him wished to take the debate and escalate it into a full fight; part of him wished to explain things to Loyd in terms so clear that even the old farmer would agree. Instead Tyler changed the subject. "What are your plans for tomorrow?"

"We'll ambush 'em at the bend, where Crack-Brady canyon heads south. I just wish I knew how many damned bandits to expect." He, too, seemed glad to have the more demanding discussion behind him.

They walked on, trudging endlessly through the darkness. After a time, Tyler found the resources to ask the question that had been simmering at the back of his mind for some time.

"About the man in that photograph; have you seen him?"

Loyd waited a while before answering. "I think I have."

"Well?"

"You say he was the Concordat ambassador here?"

"Not ambassador, but an accredited representative."

"Well, he was heading north, into the roughest part of this mountain range. He was alone, and came through here begging. We gave him a little food—dried travelling stuff, mostly—and sent him on his way. He never said who he was, and we didn't ask. It's just as well for him he didn't say, I'd guess."

"How long ago was that?"

"Seven days ... or was it eight? Seven days ago; just after we'd fought back the bandits for the second time."

"Thanks."

"Good luck finding him."

Tyler devoted his energy to walking and to thinking. *Seven days on foot, through this terrain. I'll find him. And then I'll kill him.*

Before long they arrived at a rocky promontory overlooking the main valley that led up to the town. Still high in the mountains, the valley at its lower end dropped away into sheer crags that descended yet farther, before leveling out at last into the continent's central plain. Loyd whistled aloud, two long and two short, a call that was repeated, reversed, as a countersign from the darkness ahead.

A light was uncovered, and a man stepped from a hidden tent. "Loyd! What's up?"

"The bandits will probably attack tomorrow, up Crack-Brady canyon. These two saw them from the air."

The man gave Tyler and Garvey a searching look. "Are these the two guys you captured tonight? Lewis came down here with a report about it."

"Yeah. I'm willing to trust 'em ... somewhat." Among men loyal to him, Loyd was regaining his spirits, which had sunk quite low over the course of the evening.

"All right; what's the plan?"

"We'll leave a scout force here, with some messengers, just in case, while most of us cross up to Crack-Brady. We'll set up an ambush at the bend, and wipe 'em out."

"And if your friends are lying?" the man asked, giving Tyler a meaningful glance.

"Then we'll do two things, Phillip. We'll move up Crack-Brady at top speed, and we'll still come out at the top ahead of the bandits. Then we'll kill these two with our bare hands. But I'm not worried. I think they're telling it straight."

"We'll find out, I guess."

Inside the tent, Tyler was able to get a good look at Phillip. Of average height, weight, and build, he was balding, unshaven since yesterday, round-faced and melancholy. He seemed too soft to be in a scout camp, and Tyler wondered what this Phillip had done before the war. Probably the man had stood as a clerk behind a counter in a feed store, doing little physical labor throughout his entire life. Now, fumbling with a rifle and bandoliers, Phillip looked and obviously felt like a child playing at soldier, with no real experience.

"Rolf, go get Lewis, Maynard, and Immers."

Rolf disappeared. Tyler spread his map on the card table that served the camping tent as a command table. The men bent over it busily. Jacob called Tyler off to one side.

"How do we know you aren't lying?"

"You heard Phillip and your brother. If I am, you'll kill me and my guide." He grinned. "Or you'll try."

Jacob was unmoved. "How do we know you won't get a message to the bandits, telling them that the main valley is unguarded? How do we know you aren't a goddamn spy?"

Tyler faced the man squarely and thrust out his jaw. "Jacob, you can be remarkably stupid when you want to be. Why the hell would I do it this way? With that helicopter, I could have killed off every man in your pitiful guard patrol. With this rifle, I could hold back everyone in your town, pinned down and out of range. If I were with the bandits, I'd have killed you all by now, and be working on your livestock. If you don't agree with my politics, say so. But don't you slander me, you fat-bellied son of a—"

"Tyler! Stop it." Garvey's voice was close to Tyler's ear. The others in the room either hadn't noticed or didn't care.

Tyler recognized the burning in his chest that always accompanied his vitriolic outbursts and with an effort pushed his rage back from him. It didn't matter. The fury would come over him again . . . and again . . . and again, until at last it got him killed. And in the back of his mind something sly and hidden urged him to give himself over to that killing rage. . . .

As always, the effort to regain control caused the dull ache to move from his chest to the pit of his stomach, where it sat like an indigestible meal. Saliva filled his mouth, accompanying the nausea that he felt for Jacob, for the universe, and for himself.

He didn't resist when, after a moment's indecision, Garvey lightly gripped one of his arms and ushered him outside. It struck him as a novelty that someone actually cared for his safety. It surprised him far more that that someone was Garvey.

From outside the tent, they could clearly hear the conversation within. "Where are they going?" Phillip asked.

Jacob growled, "If you ask me . . ."

"No one did, Jacob," Loyd said, his voice carefully taking the sting out of the reprimand. "We can trust them. I'm as sure of that as I've ever been sure of anything."

"You're willing to throw away everything just because you have a feeling you can trust them?"

"Sit down, Jacob. Look here . . . Is the riding trail clear, down to Crack-Brady?"

"Yeah."

Outside, in the chill darkness, Garvey sat Tyler on a boulder a few paces distant from the tent. The voices were now no more than indistinct mutterings. No stars were visible under a high, rapidly descending fogbank.

"I've been watching you since we left Camp Epsilon," Garvey said softly. "And, James, I think I've discovered something." His hand gripped Tyler's elbow. "You're bent on suicide."

Tyler said nothing, and only stared straight ahead into the pitch-black murk. His stomach and esophagus felt tight, fiery; his head ached.

"I don't know all that much about psychology," Garvey continued quietly, "but I was an educated man . . . before the war. I'm sure."

"I . . ." Tyler stammered, recalling himself.

"You're a sick man, James. How often do you kill?"

Tyler shook his head. "You're wrong." He took a deep breath. "I know what I'm doing." It sounded false, even to him.

Suicide? The coward's way out! I'm not afraid of life, or of death. I'll face both as I always have: fairly, with my gun in my hand. People shoot at me; I shoot back. I will continue to win until . . . But I won't run away.

Deeper in his mind, the part of him that never slept and that was never silent mocked him. Dim echoes of hollow laughter and of gates slamming shut accompanied the thin, imagined voice as it asked its only question. *You won't run away. What do you run toward?*

"I'll be back in a minute," he said abruptly, rising awkwardly to his feet in the darkness. Garvey made no move to stop him. Working his way through the high undergrowth of the hillside camp, he was soon gone.

It was only then that Garvey noticed that his radio was missing.

It was clipped to my belt when I left the tent. Only Tyler has had the opportunity to take it. He waited, dire thoughts circling within his head. Would Tyler dare signal a message to the bandits, telling them of the defenders' change of plans? Could he be that vindictive? By the gods that were not, something must be done! And even as he decided that, he knew that there was nothing whatever he could do.

Tyler returned a few minutes later, having dealt with whatever malicious business he had concocted. In the darkness, Garvey barely felt the feather-light brush against his belt that Tyler made while returning the radio to its clip. Garvey never would have noticed if he had not already known the device was gone.

Who to tell? Jacob? Phillip? They'd kill Tyler without bothering to listen to an explanation. Loyd? He'd be only too glad to hand the prisoner over to Jacob, who would offer kindly to take the trouble off Loyd's busy mind.

"Shall we go back inside?" Tyler asked. He sounded

horribly complacent to Garvey. He had the voice of someone who had done a great wrong without any possibility of being caught.

They entered the tent, Tyler slightly in the lead. Together, the five men spent an hour studying the map, planning the operation. Tyler's advice was shrewd, and was generally heeded. Garvey and Jacob were the only ones who retained doubts.

Finally, with a huge stretching yawn of satisfaction, Tyler suggested that the company retire until an hour before sunrise, at which time they could deploy for the ambush. All agreed, and space and bedrolls were found for the extra men. The only sounds to be heard throughout the long night were those made by the sentries as they paced sleeplessly around the perimeter of the camp.

Rude hands shook Tyler awake. Irritated, he crawled out of his bedroll, and dressed and shaved in the pearly fog. There was just enough light to march by. With a minimum of disorderly confusion, the column of some thirty men moved off along the riding trail toward Crack-Brady canyon.

Tyler took a position halfway through the column; Garvey followed nearly upon his employer's footsteps. He kept pace mechanically as they marched through the gray tunnel formed by head-high vegetation flanking the trail. The fine dust of the trail was damp from the thick fog, and fine beads of moisture were visible in the scratchy brush to the side. Tyler could only see a few meters ahead of him, which, he found, limited the world to a small sphere floating in timeless space. Gradually, however, the light grew stronger, and in places the trail grew steeper.

Finally the column climbed above the fog altogether, and Tyler's face was warmed by the direct red rays of the rising sun. Without his knowing it, the trail had swerved about until they were facing east, although at the top of the next hill it edged back toward the south, as expected.

The order came back from the head of the column to spread out and advance through the thick brush in a skirmish line formation. It seemed most natural for Tyler to take to the uphill direction, with Garvey following the path he blazed.

"Aren't you going to get your rifle ready?" Garvey asked, somewhat out of breath.

"It's okay where it is," Tyler answered, absently glancing at the heavy weapon as it lay slung over his back.

"They're evidently afraid we're going to contact the enemy sometime soon."

"I don't think we're far from our ambush site. When the land starts to drop away, we'll know we're descending into the canyon." He thought a minute. "Although we'll be contacted sooner than Loyd or Phillip expect."

Garvey stopped. "What do you mean by that?"

"What I mean is . . ." Tyler also stopped. An echo of a short volley of gunfire resounded from ahead. Nothing more could be heard.

"I guess they've already been contacted."

"Tyler! What . . . ?"

Five men appeared suddenly. They weren't dressed in the tattered rags of hill bandits, but rather in . . .

"Disarm!" snapped the voice of the nearest.

"Right on time," Tyler said heartily.

"Are you Tyler?"

"I am."

"Captain Leyden, 2nd Battalion, 4427th Marines, Colonel Teiche commanding." The man paused for a moment. "I guess you're in charge."

They were dressed in the chain-plastic battle armor of Concordat Marines.

Tyler and the unspeaking Garvey were given into the charge of a young Marine, who conducted them over the rocky ground until they hit the trail. From there another man took them down into the bottom of Crack-Brady canyon.

Across the stream, Colonel Teiche had placed his

mobile command in a small clearing. In one tent Teiche
and his communication gear monitored the fire-brigade
invasion; in another tent complex the bandits and
disarmed farmers received medical treatment and a
hot, heavy meal.

Hovering silently two meters above the meadow that
ran in a strip along the rapid stream, the landing craft
waited patiently—assault door gaping wide, loading
ramp down. Nearby, two men hauled on a lanyard,
erecting yet another tent at the end of the small row.

As Tyler let himself into the commander's tent, he
was met by Colonel Teiche, and by Loyd, Rolf, and
Jacob. Garvey followed discreetly.

"Commander Tyler," Teiche intoned, repressing a
grin. "Your Battalion, sir."

"You no good son of a—" Jacob began; an NCO
swatted him to silence, cautioning him without malice
but without sympathy.

"What have you done, James Tyler?" Loyd asked.

"I believe I've just founded an advance base camp.
What letter are we up to?"

"Ran out of letters of the alphabet," Teiche said
cheerfully. "This will be camp Forty-seven."

"All right. You'll be getting foodstuffs from up the
stream where the three roads come together. The town
is Marano; it's on your map. You'll be getting all the
power you need from their buried fusion generator.
You can build a road in . . . ?"

Teiche glanced at the map. "Two days."

"Okay. We probably won't need more than a Company for guard and patrol duty. The new citizens of
Marano won't be any trouble once they're acclima-
tized. You'll have to build barracks, pipelines, sewers
. . . hell, you know your business better than I. Who's
going to be your prefect?"

"I thought I'd use Captain Leyden, until things cool
down, when I'll throw in some lieutenant as his relief.
The rest of the Battalion will go back up into our
damned, cramped transport in holding orbit." His tone
became conspiratorial. "We held a lottery between the

Companies. The Company that disarmed the most locals, while injuring the fewest, gets to stay here. The Second Company won, but not by a lot."

Jacob had begun to snarl, rather gently, and the NCO watched him sharply. It was Loyd, however, who broke the peace. "What has happened? Will I be allowed to return to my home?"

Teiche and Tyler turned to the three men, each so much like the other two, yet each so different. Jacob was angry, with the bitterness of his entire life focused here. Loyd was confused, lost, afraid. And if Loyd, Rolf's lord and master, the central upholding pillar of the young man's life, was at a loss, what could the son do but sit motionless, staring ahead of himself and anticipating nothing. His world, after all, had just come to an end . . . for the second time. Garvey, who had been listening carefully, had deduced the answer, and tried not to face the three townsmen as they had it explained to them.

"See here," Teiche began. "We're putting an end to your pointless squabbles over your next day's meal. What you probably don't know . . ."

Beating the prisoners when they're helpless had never appealed to Tyler. Gently he interrupted. "Take it easy. They've been through a lot."

"Hm. Quite right. Care to carry on?"

Jacob covered his fear with bitter rage. Loyd watched the world, which he'd built in five weeks, crumble about him. Rolf watched the shadows crawl across the tent floor, his mind overawed by the events of the past month and the past day.

"I said that I was bringing the Concordat into this. Didn't you believe me? Did you think I was speaking no more than abstractly, about the far future?"

The line was pointless; the three sat unmoving, unmoved. A trapped, helpless feeling flooded into Tyler; a choking sensation gripped him. Always before he had lashed out at things that resisted his will. With these people, however, brutal language would only stiffen their inner resistance.

"You have enough food to feed everyone in this valley. Isn't that true, Mr. Shayler?"

Loyd stirred. "We haven't got . . . all that much."

"You used to have. What changed?"

"When . . . it happened, I couldn't get feed grain . . ."

"But now you can. We're rebuilding the roads down to the lowlands."

"The lowlands are all dead."

"They think the same about you up here. Although they realize you'll have escaped the bombings, they have assumed that your mountains are overrun with bandits."

"Well, weren't we?"

"The bandits are people that might have moved up here to live, if things hadn't gone wrong. Some of them were tourists, who used to spend their money on your foodstuffs. If things had happened differently, you yourself might have been forced to become a bandit leader."

"I never . . ."

Tyler didn't answer his objection immediately. Instead, he let Loyd think the subject through for a time. The farmer was smart enough to see that the difference between bandit and honest man was merely one of circumstances. To survive, Loyd would indeed have set himself up as a bandit leader—and a very effective one, certainly.

The bustling business of the advance camp sounded as a dim murmur beyond the breeze-waved walls of the tent. The NCO guarding the prisoners had let his attention flag, and was studying a native form of insect life. Bored, the man crushed the tiny creature and wiped his hands on his tunic. Tyler saw this and thought about it, while watching Loyd in his own turmoil of decision.

Tyler could only marvel at the beastheadedness of his species. Loyd sat in deep thought, trying to chart the course of his tiny settlement for the years to come; Jacob suppressed his anger and resentment, unaware that all he had ever wanted from the day was to kill several bandits; Rolf hovered at the edge of a cata-

tonic trance—unsure, unguided, and feeling his helplessness not as a pang, but as a warm blanket of
apathy. And behind them, insensitive to their agony, a
man crushed tiny winged insects in order to pass the
time between direct orders.

"The road will let feed trucks come up from the
valleys?" Loyd asked after an extended pause.

"Yes. At first, you'll pay with foodstuffs. After a
time, we'll put together a monetary system and issue
scrip."

"I'll be able to get the machine parts I might need?"

From where? Tyler thought. "I suppose that Horla
continent will be doing some exporting . . ."

"And at what price?"

"Exorbitant. One of our biggest problems will be to
keep the Horlan governments from taking advantage
of all of Theury."

"None of my concern."

"Possibly. We'll be helping to keep things orderly."

"And I'll have to quarter these bandits on my ranch?
Feed them? Take care of them? How will I know—"

"You'll have to feed them, give them a tap on your
power plant, and put them to work where they'll be of
most use. They'll build their own quarters, and you'll
fix them up with land to clear, just to keep them busy.
We'll integrate them into your economy as fast as we
can."

"How will I know they're not stealing? How will I
control them?"

"That's what our prefect will be seeing to. You'll
have a Company of Concordat Marines to feed also,
and if you've never seen hungry men, you'll see them
now."

"But they will be leaving . . . someday?"

"Yes. The sooner you get your operation under control, the faster we'll pull out."

"And what about the damned green flag flying over
our courthouse?"

Tyler faced him and answered honestly. "That might
happen. It's what I'm on this world to determine. My

report will be read by the Foreign Secretary, and will be summarized before the Praesidium. Their word is law."

Jacob's anger had by now faded into a heartsick resentment—Tyler knew the feeling well—and if he wasn't listening with an open heart, at least he was listening. Rolf, however, sat watching but not seeing, present but not hearing. Tyler addressed his last comments to Loyd, hoping that Rolf would understand when, someday, the words were recalled to mind.

"You've got a lot of rebuilding to do. You won't complete it in your lifetime, or in your son's. But by the time his sons have inherited your farm and ranch, it will be an establishment that neither of us would recognize. Because we're putting an advance camp by your town, you'll have the best direct aid we can give you. You'll have satellite weather photos, chemical shipments direct from Horla, and a guaranteed market for your produce. We've also given you the equivalent of slave labor for the time it takes the bandits to become full citizens. Your farm will fill all the valleys for a long distance about you; you and your son will share in rebuilding this continent."

"But will it be ours, or will it belong to the Concordat?" Loyd asked quietly.

"I hope that it can be both. The farm, its buildings and machines, will always be yours. The land will be yours, and the livestock. If this world becomes a member of the Concordat, the only thing you'll lose is the right to ruin your investment through bad choices . . . which you don't want to do anyway. The market, because it will be monitored, will be far less susceptible to upsets and profit-destroying fluctuations. Have you ever had an entire good year's income absorbed by a bad year? Have you ever grown grains when the market couldn't pay you fairly for them? If the Concordat moves directly to integrate this world into its economy, you'd never again need to worry about that."

"What kind of say will I have in the Concordat's final decision?"

Tyler's face was sad as he answered, "None whatsoever."

"What am I to do?"

"Run your farm. Let it grow. Obey our prefect. Be equally fair to your townsmen and to the ex-bandits. Elections will be held someday, I guarantee it. Then, you'll have your say. Someday, your son will be a very powerful man."

Loyd had no answer. After a time, Tyler signaled to Colonel Teiche.

"I've got an investigative mission to complete. I'll leave things in your hands."

"Call us in again if you need to," Teiche said with subdued cheer. He detailed a squad of Marines to escort Tyler and Garvey by air-car to the middle of the town where their helicopter waited.

The blue-green underbrush fell away beneath them, passing silently beneath the swift-moving air-car. Tyler followed Crack-Brady canyon with his eyes, noting how it indeed led swiftly and not too steeply up to the town. In a few minutes the driver swooped low over the concrete lip of the town dam and moved across the still water at high speed. Rising again, they circled the town, busy now with troop activity. Already the skeletal frames of new barracks were being thrown together in a vacant field near the farm buildings. The second Battalion's second Company would be living there, keeping the peace between the townsmen and the people they'd so recently warred with. The town proper stood a little to the side, where the roads met. The Marine engineers would have the bridges repaired soon, and reroute the roads to join with the many lowlands advance camps.

There, at the exact junction of the three roads, three bored Marines stood watch over Tyler's helicopter. The driver of the air-car set the machine down smoothly near it, and leaped nimbly out to speak with the nearest guardsman.

"Good luck, Commander," one of them called. Tyler waved absently as he and Garvey climbed into the helicopter's cockpit.

"Where to, James?" Garvey asked quietly, once the doors were shut.

"Highlands north of here. I've got a guy to kill."

Garvey said nothing. In a moment the harsh roar of the engine cut off all conversation, and the machine bounded roughly into the cool air.

The Communications and Electromagnetic Effects ship *Graphein*, Commerce Secretary Redmond's roving headquarters vessel, fell out of jumpspace with an easy precision, high above the pearlescent globe of Horltheur. Not far distant followed the imposing bulk of the Navy Battleship *Fair Phyllis*. Within seconds, radio communication was established between the two, linking Redmond with Grand Admiral de la Noue.

"Admiral."

"Secretary."

Adrian Redmond was a slim, small man, who tended to dress to the occasion with a precise flair that no one about him could quite seem to match. His close-cropped reddish-blond hair was stylishly offset by a trim, sharp beard and a well-tended moustache. No one had ever claimed to have seen him without headgear of some sort, the exact nature of which varied drastically from week to week. As de la Noue regarded him over the viewscreen, she could see today's apparel included a skullcap of deep inky green worn well off to the left side. Belying his frivolous manner of dress—frivolous, that is, to those who were not in the know when it came to the currents of high fashion—was his businesslike attitude toward work. He ran the Concordat's economy as if his life depended upon it, regarding even the most insignificant fluctuation with completely unwarranted seriousness. The upset to interstellar commerce caused by the recent nuclear war on the planet Horltheur was grave enough to mandate his direct intervention. Travelling as always in a ship that was a mobile nerve center, he could see to things here while maintaining his link to as much of the Concordat's vital dealings as could be arranged.

Grand Admiral Jennifer de la Noue, sitting in the air-conditioned bridge of the *Fair Phyllis*, was pleasantly aware of Redmond's talent, secure in the knowledge that the economic end of the matter was in good hands. Redmond, on his end of the link, saw de la Noue as a truly handsome woman, with long blond hair and a charming face. Her uniform, however . . . He couldn't help but wince, if only mentally, at that harsh, efficient red outfit with the white piping. Her form deserved no less than eight yards of flowing yellow-gold silk, with a coronet of blooming orcranthani blossoms . . . He lost himself in a vision of her face beneath such a garland, her high cheekbones and wide hazel eyes blending with the colors of the costume that his artist's mind created without effort.

The fantasy was all too brief. Still, the uniform looked good on her, if only because anything would look good on her. Redmond dropped the speculation, not without regret, and bent his mind to the gigantic effort that lay before him.

"My display indicates that our fleet is in perfect formation, although my instruments were strained to the uttermost to compensate for the extraordinary mass of your Battleship. Was it necessary to bring it along?"

De la Noue smiled at the thought of bringing a million-ton spacecraft—complete with Marine division and Fighter complement—as a keepsake. It amused her primarily because it was true. A Light Cruiser would have sufficed, and would have been less expensive. But just now it was important that she be thought of as the true head of the fleet, and she wanted to spread the impression that where de la Noue went, the fleet followed. She had survived the recent statutory and legal battles by forcing her will upon the Supreme Council of Sectors, but the lesson still needed to be underlined: The Grand Admiral and the fleet are inseparable, and to unseat one is to dangerously weaken the second.

"I'm sure your instruments are versatile enough to play the role of jump coordinator for larger fleets than

this." She knew full well that the jump coordinating
computers on board the *Fair Phyllis* wouldn't have
handled the transition with the micrometric precision
that Redmond's supercomputers had. Balancing the
stresses of jumpspace against the torsion created by
even a single ship was a complex task. This fleet
boasted, besides the Battleship and the Electronics
ship, a sizeable backup force of Cruisers, Scouts, and
Transports, as well as eight direly needed Hospital
ships. Overall, the fleet was full to capacity with the
varied supplies that Redmond had decided the devastated portions of the world below needed most.

"Come along, Secretary," de la Noue suggested. "Let's
establish orbit." The fleet, bearing two of the six most
highly placed individuals in the entire Concordat, moved
planetward. Within seven hours the 104 ships were
spread in a tight formation orbiting the scarred world.
Soon, protocol messages were flashing rapidly between
the sovereign Horlan nations on the untouched continent and the Battleship. Permission was granted without delay for the Transports to begin offloading supplies
to the ruins of Theury continent.

"Hello, Mr. Redmond," de la Noue greeted the Secretary formally as he stepped aboard her flagship. "When
do we begin cargo shuttling?"

"Well," Redmond began, looking about him in interest at the functional command bridge of the Battleship, "I find that the main reconstruction camp is in
the charge of one Commander Denis, a Navy chap.
You might want to have a talk with him, seeing that
you speak his language."

De la Noue nodded, recalling that detail from the
files she'd read through on the trip here.

Her crew quickly established a video contact, and
within seconds the two aboard the Battleship were
speaking with the Commander.

"Grand Admiral." Denis saluted. "I'm somewhat
surprised."

"Why?"

"It just seems that this is a bit of a local storm that
shouldn't affect the Praesidium at all."

"Look here, young man," Redmond said without heat. "Do you realize how much this war has disrupted the local infrastructure? Can you appreciate how much this has me and my staff concerned? The effects will be felt in every market in the entire sphere."

De la Noue couldn't help but smile at the concerned expression on Denis's face. "But with Secretary Redmond personally overseeing every phase of the recovery, we can surely relax securely," she replied.

Denis was not reassured. "Seriously, Admiral, Secretary, how bad are the effects? I don't know that much about economics . . ."

Redmond waved a hand dismissingly, starting to say, "Oh, it won't be anything . . ." at the same time that de la Noue herself grew serious, and began, "We can't be sure . . ." Denis's worried expression did not change.

Redmond shot a questioning look at de la Noue and began afresh. "The fluctuations will be felt throughout the sphere. But any variables will be damped out with extreme rapidity. Even the nearest planets won't really feel much. What I'm most concerned about, if the truth be known, is reestablishing a working economy on this world. That is what's most vital, not to the Concordat as a whole, but directly to this world. I'm here to see to it in person, so that the hell this planet has been through will affect the least possible number of people." He paused. "I don't know why the Grand Admiral is here, but I'm sure she has her reasons."

De la Noue smiled. "I'm here because for the first time in my term of office nothing larger is happening that needs my attention."

"I've been against spending money on military programs for quite some time, myself," Redmond said mischievously. "It really doesn't contribute anything to the wealth of the sphere."

Commander Denis kept his silence, warily watching the rare sight of two Praesidium members in good-natured debate.

De la Noue's expression turned serious once again.

"Commander Denis, have you had any success in finding the legitimate government of the areas you're trying to save?"

"None whatever, Admiral." His face was grave. "The highest official that we've found was a sub-regional representative to an under-council. I can't see dealing with him as the legal leader of the entire continent."

"This world is legally independent of the Concordat—"

"Idiotic. Damn fool policy."

Redmond's sharp comment took de la Noue by surprise. His expression revealed his disgust at what he considered the foolishness of thus dividing sovereignty.

"It was granted to them by Praesidium decree in 778," de la Noue said easily, "and ratified by the Supreme Council later that year. This world is an island, free in the midst of the Concordat, even though we surround it. We're obligated to respect this freedom. That, Commander, is why you will be required to watch carefully to see that none of your actions violate local laws." She shook her head, smoothing back her hair. "For instance, even though it might be necessary, you can't declare martial law."

Denis shrugged. "That was the first thing I did. If you want me to pull my troops out and let these people kill each other for scraps of food . . .

"Admiral," he continued helplessly, "I understand and agree with what you say, but I really have no choice. You'd have to come down here and see what we have to deal with. And anyway, I've got the permission of every one of the Horlan nations to do whatever I feel is necessary to help this continent."

"But the Horlan nations don't have the legal right to give you that power." De la Noue leaned forward, staring into the viewscreen. "I know what you need to do, and I know what obstacles you face. We just need to see that we aren't charged with violating the treaty that gives them independence."

"Charged by whom? There's no one here to protest."

"Well, for what it's worth, you've got official Praesidium sanction to do just about anything you need to help this continent. And of course you've been working on the rescue longer than I have."

"Does my martial law remain in force?"

De la Noue considered that for a moment. "If the Horlan states don't mind . . ."

"They've given me official sanction."

"I guess the survivors are safer under your protection than they would be without it. Very well. You continue in charge, and I'll drop down to review your procedures. I suppose that little will need changing."

Denis looked at her inquisitively. "I thought that the Praesidium was considering incorporating this world into the Concordat."

"Why would you think that?" De la Noue knew that some Praesidium members wanted to annex the world, but she thought that the matter hadn't gotten very far beyond that. Although, she had to admit, some of her staff did have strong opinions about it. Her intelligence chief, Admiral Higgins, upon learning of the war here, had argued quite persuasively for reintegrating the world into the overall sphere, so that it could be most effectively protected from future insanity.

"Well, I had a Navy officer through here recently, investigating whether or not to bring the world back into full membership, and if so, how best to do it."

"Do you have a copy of his authorization?"

"He was from Exonidas city, Horla continent. If you want, I can try to access it from their computer . . ."

"I'll take care of it from here." De la Noue laughed. "I've got a slightly higher authorization code."

"Yes, ma'am."

De la Noue considered. Quite possibly the man had been sent by Higgins's order . . . but if it was an investigative mission on that sensitive a matter of policy, wouldn't he have asked her first? Or was Foreign Secretary Vissenne suborning her officers already? That one certainly had no love for the idea of independent principalities in the midst of the Concordat. Yes, she would definitely look into the investigator's orders once she concluded her business with Denis.

"Using the cargo shuttles from this Battleship," Redmond suggested, "I can have some million and a half tons of supplies unloaded inside two days. If you could spare a man who could help me match cargos with landing sites . . ."

Denis was all too happy to comply; soon Redmond and a supplies officer were busily copying figures and allocations into each other's computers.

"That's the best thing—the only good thing—about Navy Battleships: lots of cargo shuttles," Redmond said over his shoulder to de la Noue.

She grinned. "See? We can carry things besides combat troops."

"Marines!" Redmond scowled playfully. "I'd never let my daughter marry one."

De la Noue ignored him, and turned back to Denis's image on her small viewscreen. "I *do* think it's important to find a real representative of the Theury governments to deal with. If the only elected survivor is that sub-regional lawmaker . . ."

"Well, he's merely the highest placed official we've definitely contacted. As of last week, our best bet was one Potok Empellimin, a military security prefect with Vistheur." Denis turned aside to consult a datascreen. "He was known to have been up in the mountains, when things went bad . . . hm." He looked apologetically back at the screen. "We've got a new listing. It seems he's dead."

"Do what you can, Commander. I'll be arriving with the second wave of shuttles to Emergency city."

"Very well, Admiral." Denis saluted, and broke off contact.

De la Noue frowned. An official investigator? She used a radio link to access the files of the Concordat spaceport at Exonidas city. Once her authorization was okayed, the material she desired was relayed to her reading screen. There was indeed an officer, with the rank of Commander, who was investigating ways to end this world's sovereignty. His name and an I.D. photo were attached.

De la Noue's eyes widened in surprise. "James Tyler," she whispered, and tapped an intercom key. "Records Division."

"Yes?" a clerk answered.

"Is Commodore Steldan to hand?"

"I'll get him."

"Yes, ma'am?" said Athalos Steldan after a moment. Plainly he was wondering what his next assignment would be.

"Do you recognize this person?" de la Noue asked, transmitting the data sheet to Steldan's viewscreen.

Commodore Steldan raised an eyebrow. "I should say I do. He only tried to kill me three times."

"It says here that he's been assigned to look into ways of taking this planet into the Concordat. The problem is, I never made that assignment."

"According to this, he's in the Support Branch, Legal Division, which puts him under Higgins . . . who's not aboard, is he?"

"No. He's still looking into things back in the Sonallan Outreach."

"Do I understand correctly that the mission Tyler's on should never have been authorized?"

"Not without my specific okay. And I'd probably have checked with the Foreign Secretary before finalizing it."

Steldan gazed speculatively at a point just above the video pickup. "The last I'd heard of Tyler, he was in prison."

"That's right," de la Noue agreed. "And I'd like to know just who had him released."

"I'll start looking into it immediately." He smiled. "And I was told that a career in the Records Division would be dull."

"Not in *our* Navy," de la Noue agreed. Signing off, she let her smile fade as she reread Tyler's data sheet. It contained very little real information.

James Tyler, she thought grimly. She'd only seen him once—in the crowded chamber where she had been presiding over an investigative committee. Steldan had entered the room with a startling revelation about then-current Grand Admiral Telford, and hot on his heels was Tyler with a gun in his hand. A quick-thinking officer had shot and wounded Tyler before the assassin could kill Steldan. Later, it had been proven that the would-be killer was in Telford's pay; the shake-up that followed had reached every level of the Navy.

De la Noue had to grin at the memory: Suddenly that meeting had turned from a dull repetition of old accusations to a brief but bloody firefight. She, too, had been told that working in the Operations Branch of the Navy would be a dull task.

"Signal a passenger shuttle," she said into the inter-com. "I'll be leaving for Emergency city immediately."

Standing, she looked about the bridge, appreciating its orderly discipline. The main engines were nearly to their shut-down configuration; standby systems were operating normally.

She exited through the Fleet Command Bridge, a small corridor to the aft of the Command Bridge. A cross-corridor and an elevator took her quickly to the boat deck, where her aide and two security officers awaited her.

"Ready, Lee?"

"All set, ma'am."

They entered the shuttle, and Lee stepped forward to the pilot's compartment. Minutes later the small craft kicked itself out through a large bay door, shot edgewise between two of the *Fair Phyllis'* titanic ar-mor plates, and rolled over for a long dive into the thick atmosphere of Horltheur.

The great ship dwindled behind them, until at last the billion-ton war vessel was little more than a glint-ing shaft against the stars. Half an hour later the shuttle grounded at the Emergency city landing field.

Lee, after final-checking the craft's instruments, wan-dered back into the passenger compartment and re-leased the doors, opening the boat to the gloomy skies and landscape of Theury continent.

"Good landing, Lee," de la Noue commented as she descended the stair.

"Thank you, ma'am."

The two Marines descended next, and Lee watched them with hidden contempt. They'd hit planets aboard landing craft, assault boats whose internal anticoncussion fields were required to keep the passengers alive. What could they possibly know about precision landings?

Shrugging, Lee sealed the craft, and let herself down the stairway with the aplomb of one whose duty it is to ferry a Grand Admiral.

Not long afterward—*one does not keep a Grand Admiral waiting,* thought Lee—Commander Denis and some of his staff arrived from the office building to one side of the field.

After a few formalities, Denis took them on a brief walking tour of inspection. Within minutes de la Noue detected a haunting difference between the attitude of the Navy personnel working here and that of the survivors. The difference was perhaps subtly expressed, but it was real and nearly uniform: The survivors really no longer cared. Two men dug a trench with an automated tool. One of them detested the work, and mopped often at his brow with a cloth. The other went about the labor with an abstracted, machinelike insensitivity. Farther along, a team sprayed paint over a wire fence. The Navy people went about it in practiced, even strokes, reviewing their work now and again; the survivors just laid it on and moved over to the next section.

The city was reasonably large, considering its age, and showed the typical Concordat flair for advance planning. Energy, drainage, water, communication, and roads were all integrated into a pleasing, functional design. Bunkhouses, cafeterias, and storehouses, all prefabricated, were arranged in neat rows by subsection, with open spaces for group assembly alternating with close ranks of gray buildings. One team had been sent by truck beyond the perimeter of the destruction to bring back trees and other greenery. Replanted, they did lend some slight cheer to the city.

It was no use. Cutting squarely along the border between rescuers and survivors was a gloom that could not be dispelled. The survivors all felt a quiet apathy. They would never again know certainty. They could no longer dare to care for anything, for fear of losing it, too.

There had to be exceptions, de la Noue felt. Some hardy individuals who had recovered from their shock and were throwing themselves into the back-breaking labor of restoration, perhaps even with a willful cheer. For decades, this was going to be a land where an ambitious man or woman could build a fortune, if not an empire. She looked about her for evidence of determined, struggling citizens of the area, who had not let the hell just past break their spirit.

She didn't find any.

"Over there"—Commander Denis broke into de la Noue's reverie—"we've got a nursery set up, with dedicated local staffers to take care of the children. It's almost as therapeutic for the adults as it is for the youngsters. Gives them something to care for and to worry about beyond their own subjective anguish. The children—most of them—will be all right, I suppose. It's the young adults that my staff psychologists are most worried about." He had an effective, if crisp, lecturing tone. De la Noue listened, while her eyes roved over the varied sights of the city.

"Over there, to the west, we've got the hospitals and physical therapy wards. The worst cases are in orbit, of course, in weightless burn treatment. I'm most exceptionally grateful that your hospital ships were able to arrive as swiftly as they did," said Commander Denis.

"The notion's fairly old, almost a matter of tradition," de la Noue explained. "Give the doctors their heads, and little can go wrong. From war experience, they know how to deal with flash burns."

"Even with their aid, we had something like sixty percent burn victim fatalities, simply because the ships couldn't get here in time. Since they arrived, the percentage, I'm told, will drop to—quite literally—zero."

"The worst cases . . ." de la Noue began, and let it drop. The worst cases had died long ago.

"Everyone we can, we treat planetside, so that they can get some visitors. I'd have thought it would lower morale to see, um, bandaged survivors moving about, but instead, we've been able to use it to good effect. It brings out the cooperative instinct in people."

They passed a neatly tended graveyard, where, de la Noue assumed, the people were interred who had survived the war itself, only to succumb to burns or infection before the rescue effort could be fairly begun.

"The rains that came in the days after were a help, in a number of ways," Denis continued after a time. "Deaths due to exposure went up a bit, but it helped put out timber and prairie fires, and the fresh water saved a good many people." Pointing to a large round storage tank, he continued, "That's our water supply now, so we're no longer dependent on the rain. There's a pipeline stretching just over that rise to the bay, where we've installed a desalination reactor, putting out, um, six hundred liters a minute. It also turns out nine percent of our electric power."

After a pause, during which de la Noue exhibited no hurry to get on with other business, Denis wandered with her and her three companions up to a low hilltop overlooking the newly surfaced spaceport landing field. De la Noue conferred quietly with Denis as the cool onshore breeze fanned the party; Lee gave the port facilities a professional looking-over and privately judged them acceptable. The two Marines, new to the sea, gazed out at the ribbon of blue and exchanged wondering comments about the endless expanses of water.

Every two minutes the silence was shattered by the roar of a cargo shuttle as it settled gingerly onto the field's surface, where ground tractors would attach themselves and tow the heavily laden ships away. From another quarter of the field, the empty shuttles rose skyward, thrown clear by their own gravitic boosters.

"We don't have a boost-grid installed, of course. If we did, we don't have the power. It seems somewhat wasteful of fuel . . ."

"Fuel's free," de la Noue laughed.

Denis grinned crookedly. "Yes, ma'am. We have an ocean full. Still . . ." After a time, during which several shuttles were broached and partially emptied, he sighed. "My staff is probably getting along perfectly well without me, but I do think I should be getting back. Before that, though, I'm afraid I do have news."

De la Noue looked at him, saying nothing.

"The first thing is that the elected official I mentioned, the sub-regional lawmaker, has, um, committed suicide. It's been happening to a lot of the survivors . . ." He took a deep breath. "Well, anyway, the other point was that the gentleman I mentioned earlier, Potok Empellimin, may still be alive. *May* be. It seems that the entry verifying his death was spurious."

"Spurious?"

"I think that your Commander Tyler might have put it in."

"Why would he have done that?"

Denis shrugged. "I've been thinking about that. It seems—"

"And he's not *my* Commander Tyler," de la Noue said vehemently.

"Um. Well, it seems that he pulled a photo of this Empellimin, and then took off into the region that we had listed as Empellimin's last known whereabouts."

"I don't want to sound accusative," she responded carefully, "but why didn't you mention this earlier?"

"It didn't seem vital. Empellimin's status is still quite questionable."

"What you didn't know—what you couldn't have known—is that Commander Tyler may well be an assassin."

"There's a radio just this way," Denis said, and set off at a brisk walk. De la Noue and her bewildered team followed.

A short distance away, beyond a cluster of low buildings on the other side of the hill from the spaceport, stood a two-building communications center. Denis held the door wide for de la Noue to enter.

She motioned for the two Marine guards to stand watch outside the cramped interior of the radio room. As she entered with Lee, a radioman greeted her. The man realized at once that something serious was happening; he relinquished his seat after a glance at Denis, who had entered and shut the door.

Lee slid onto the swivel chair and glanced over the equipment. She flipped a few toggles, and punched in a trial combination frequency.

Denis interrupted carefully. "He's in a helicopter up in the Vistheur area. May I . . . ?" He bent forward and, by tapping a sequence into the keyboard, called a frequency to the data screen just to the radio's left. "Try to raise him on ninety-four."

Lee complied and within a few minutes received an answer.

De la Noue grasped the microphone. "Is this Commander James Tyler?"

The filtered voice responded—a voice that de la Noue remembered well from their brief confrontation.

"I am he."

"This is a direct order from the Grand Admiral. Return here at once."

"Grand Admiral de la Noue?"

"Speaking."

"I'm sorry; your authority doesn't extend quite this far. As long as you're in the area, look up my travelling orders."

"I have just given you new orders. As Grand Admiral I have full authority—"

"Wrong. File Black Book, code nineteen. Look it up. And it won't do you any good to try to zero in on this transmission; it's being relayed through an automatic satellite station."

"Commander—"

"I'd love to stay and talk, but that wouldn't do, would it? Tyler out."

The transmission ceased. Lee looked inquisitively at her superior, who was at a loss.

Commander Denis looked up from a data screen. "Black Book, code nineteen. It's a security file over at Exonidas spaceport, and I haven't got the authority to open it."

"Find him," de la Noue said harshly. "Get me all the data you can on Empellimin, Tyler, Black Book—whatever the hell that may be—and get it to me up on my flagship."

De la Noue, her aide Lee, and Athalos Steldan sat about a small situations table on the electronics deck of the *Fair Phyllis*. Before each of them was a small stack of bound documents. Lee eyed hers unhappily.

"Operation Black Book," Steldan began gloomily. "It seems to be older than any of us; there's no clear record of who founded it. First Secretary Todut could have, but . . . anyway, it's an assassination ring. And it's ours, sort of."

"What do you mean?" Lee asked.

"First, it was *hell* breaking the security interlocks on that file. That idiot file-guard computer had no intention of recognizing the Grand Admiral's authority. I had a little better luck, probably because I'm in the Intelligence branch. It finally turned out that Commander Tyler is directly responsible to Admiral Higgins of Naval Intelligence."

"But I never authorized the program," de la Noue objected. "How could it be running?"

"It seems to be an Intelligence inside job. Higgins found the entire system ready for him when he took over from Horst—"

"And he never told me." De la Noue's expression of anger arose from her sense of betrayal. Mentally, Steldan wrote Higgins out of any future calculations. The demand for his resignation would be moving through channels fairly soon . . .

"I doubt that your predecessor knew the full extent of the operation either."

"Telford?" De la Noue's face hardened. "Of course he knew."

Steldan remained thoughtful. "I'm not sure. There were times that it seemed Horst had power over him. Only slightly, to be sure, but it was there."

"We need to know everything about it. Find out who founded the damned thing, who runs it, and how to take it apart."

"Will you want the individual operatives arrested?" Lee asked. "We don't want them selling their services to another master, I hope."

"That's right. They'll be tried for their crimes, and so will Admiral Higgins."

"The operation," Steldan interposed quietly, "although illegal, was no doubt formed for reasons of necessity."

"Are you defending it?" de la Noue demanded.

"I know that at least three other members of the Praesidium have extralegal agencies in their employ. I know that at least one of these involves an assassination subsection."

De la Noue glared at him in disgust. "If I could, I'd publicize that statement. If I were strong enough, I'd face the entire Praesidium down on this point. Just because I can't do that is no reason I should abide such an atrocity of my own."

Steldan met her gaze. "Part of the reason the other Praesidium members *are* so strong is their willingness to use the tools of strength. Legality—"

"Is absolutely *first* among my considerations. Commodore Steldan, you will help me dismantle that operation. I won't support it, and I won't have you defending it."

"I understand."

"Do you disagree?"

Steldan gave that some thought. "Partially. Not enough to fight you about it."

"I see."

To prevent the conversation from progressing any further in that direction, Lee asked, "What about the third of these reports? The one on Empellimin?"

De la Noue took a deep breath and drew the report out of the small stack before her. "All right. What about him?"

Steldan gestured at his copy of the report with a casual wave of his hand. "Not too much survived the war; not on this continent. From Horlan accounts, I was able to put together this much: Potok Empellimin was a second Military Security Prefect for Vistheur. When the international tensions on Theury continent flared up, he seems to have committed some serious blunder—or act of war; we can't know—setting off the full warfaring power of each of the five Theuran nations.

"He was rabidly anti-Concordat. One account says he was known to fly into a frenzy at the sight of anything in green and silver. That was his particular grudge against Saftheur, for instance. Their flag was green and gold—too similar for his tastes, it would seem."

"What pattern?" Lee asked, intrigued.

"Quite ornate, unlike ours. Green, two killing-beasts facing, feet planted, in gold."

Lee said nothing, but her confusion was plain. *Why would anyone put depictions of wild beasts on his flag?*

"Anyway," Steldan continued, "he angrily resented the terms of the treaty that gave this world independence. He pointed out, time and again, that it cut the world off from any colonization of other worlds, even within the system, let alone about other stars. If he'd had the capability, I don't doubt that he'd have waged war on us long ago. Instead, his aggression and ambition were the direct cause of the death of this continent."

"That explains a lot," de la Noue agreed. "Higgins, as often as he spoke of annexing this world *before* the blow-up, would never accept the idea of this Empellimin in charge."

"That seems to be it. He had an assassin to hand, so he sent our dear Mr. Tyler out with orders to remove the threat to his ideals of unification."

"Can we stop it?"

"Not long after you had that unproductive conversation with Tyler, shipboard scanners picked up the helicopter. It had been abandoned."

"Can we find him in any other way? His body heat would show, certainly."

"I've got the entire telescopy deck working on that, full time. We've also got two platoons of Marines on one-man gravity skimmers combing the area directly. They're in touch with the telescopes, and with each other . . . but there's a lot of country down there, with many good places to hide."

"I suppose there are also quite a few wandering survivors in the area."

"Yes; hundreds. Worst of all, of course, is that James Tyler is an incredibly competent man."

De la Noue flared. "You don't need to go praising him! He's a dangerous lunatic! When he's captured, I've got a court martial waiting for him. Maybe even a death sentence."

"Yes, ma'am," Steldan whispered.

After a moment she relented. "Look, just catch him. The responsibility for the rest lies with me. Trace the Black Book back to its origins and eradicate it. And don't worry."

"Yes, ma'am. The last part, naturally, is the hard one."

"Go on, Athalos; get to work."

Steldan gathered his copies of the reports and stood, saluting the Grand Admiral and nodding absently to Lee, who nodded back in silent respect. Making for the door, Steldan paused for a moment to don his cap and straighten it; then he was gone.

Parke, Solme, and Vissenne have their own forces, extralegal in nature, although generally under control, Steldan thought. *I know that Solme's agency, masquerading as a branch of the Judiciary, has assassins in its hire. I'll do what I can to stop Tyler, this time, but I'll also have to try to save his life.*

No matter what I finally report to the Grand Admiral, I find it highly likely that operation Black Book will still be functioning by this time next year.

And heaven help me, I'll likely be in charge of it.

Steldan strode along the corridors of the titanic Battleship, the war vessel that could, unopposed, strip fifty or more worlds of all life before running out of reloads. His mission was to save as many lives as he could, starting with James Tyler and Potok Empellimin. Starting with them, but not ending there.

A few will die, and many will live. Those were the words he had found as the subtitle of the documents chartering the Black Book. Hating himself for it, Steldan nevertheless agreed.

Jill Imfarland awoke by slow degrees from her drugged sleep. The bed beneath her was damp with her sweat; nothing covered her, and she looked down the length of her nakedness with a confused, if calm, incomprehension. Heat assailed her: the heat of the register constantly blowing hot air; the heat of her own body; and that of the man who lay beside her.

Slowly her reason returned to her. She remembered nothing of the past night, but it was pretty clear what had gone on while she was helpless. Or perhaps, she thought, it was possible that she had been compliant, willing, while merely very, very drunk. She felt no headache, no aftereffects, no true sickness; she felt only a heaviness, a tiredness that made even the thought of rousing herself seem beyond effort.

The heater, she decided at last, *is at too hot a setting.* Peeling herself loose from the bedsheets, she threw her legs over the side and made shift to sit upright. The sweat cascaded down her. With another effort, she stood and padded across to the temperature controls, which she twisted all the way around to cold. At last the heat-duct ceased its scorching breath.

She looked about her. The apartment was clean, well-appointed, and decorated so as to disguise its small proportions. In the corner, on the large bed, Richard Temple slept on, moving slightly as if the bedsheets chafed him. He, too, was filmed with sweat, and his hair was plastered against his head. He had about him an unsightly ungainliness, and Jill regarded his naked form with distaste. He reminded her of her customers: Eager for his own pleasure, he considered her merely a device to aid this satisfaction.

Jill's thoughts drifted to James Tyler, with his clean blond hair, cool dry skin, and unreadable face. There had been a freshness about him, a crispness that somehow reminded her of the beaches and coves of the Sea of Lamps. His eyes had been the gray of the water . . .

Shaking her head, she strode into the apartment's bathroom and filled a glass with water. Draining it merely made her aware of how foul her mouth tasted and how thirsty she was. Two more glasses restored some freshness to her.

Soon showered, shampooed, and clear-headed, Jill dressed and settled down with a magazine, waiting for Temple to revive.

The manner of his awakening was something to watch. Jill couldn't help but envy how swiftly he returned to alertness. As soon as he noticed that she was no longer beside him, he jumped to his feet, only to stop and stare at her with a momentary expression of great emotion.

She smiled weakly. What was it upon his face? She compared it to fear, rage, and guilt, and found none of these properly descriptive.

Then the moment was past, and Temple, with a charming affectation of modesty, covered himself before retreating into the bathroom.

Jill's smile faded. Examining her own emotions reassured her: She saw nothing in the man. For that, she was thankful.

But he's my link to James Tyler, and . . . Her thoughts faded in a momentary confusion. *What is James Tyler to me? Why do I feel so strongly that I love him?* It was the first time in the whole impulsive hunt that she had dared to ask herself that brutal question when nothing else could distract her from its implications.

All my life I've been led. I've never, never made a free decision. I was—her thoughts faltered—*used, used as if I were no more than a street-running animal!*

Anger and hot, helpless frustration engulfed her; she shuddered with her effort not to weep. Gradually she regained control of her emotions.

I was cast out of my home for my crime—the crime of being raped; I narrowly avoided becoming addicted to the drugs that the vice district secretes like a sweat. I was found by a man who feigned kindness, and who sold me for a small price to a flesh-shop of the lowest sort. I've been beaten, savaged, led, dragged and sold. I've been intimate with a hundred hot, hairy men. Why am I even alive?

In Lady Titania's—so fancy a name, and so slatternly an owner—I found at least one good thing: fair pay for what I must do. Sylvia and Glory think of themselves as my friends. Do they know that I dream nightly of doing . . . horrible things to them? Do they know that I would sell them as I've been sold, if as little as a month's freedom was at stake? Do they know . . . ?

She broke down in another series of shudders. The first night she had spent at Lady Titania's, sleeping alone for the first time in months, her mind had pictured Glory, whom she had met only that day. She had dreamed of torturing Glory, who had become a symbol of the house; she had dreamed of twisting the blonde girl's arm around until the shoulder separated. The visions had gone on for some time, degenerating into acts of such savage perversity that even now, nearly a year later, her mind shrunk from remembering. In the dream, Glory had been willingly receptive to any and all degradations, and Jill's inability to shame her, to put any real expression of pain upon her, had left Jill, upon waking, shivering uncontrollably with the remnants of her dream-passion.

If Glory is the best friend I have in all the worlds, how can I ever dream to think of myself as loved?

James Tyler. A soothing image in Jill's turmoil. She needed, now, to find in her own mind what she thought of him. She tried to remember his face in every detail. He had been so businesslike upon his arrival that day. He had strolled into Lady Titania's, ignoring her and her friends with a hauteur that had not disguised his awareness. He had seen her, and Glory and Sylvia also. Jill couldn't remember which of the three he had glanced most towards.

Then, the wait of just over an hour, his emergence, his audacity, his . . . what? Jill tried again to capture the fleeting image of the moment. His kiss had been warm, frank, intimate; his hands had held hers almost tenderly. He was pulling away when their eyes met. And then he had withdrawn, an unreadable and endearing expression of uncertainty had crossed his face . . . and Jill had fallen in love.

He may be a boorish, cloddish bastard. But someone like that wouldn't have wondered, after he'd dared, what and why he had done. He dared . . . and then, a moment later, became aware. I won't stop until I meet him again!

If it required her to put up with Richard Temple, then so be it. She put all thoughts from her, and rubbed her tired eyes. Not long after, Temple emerged, and dressed himself in silence.

"I'd expected that you'd have left already," he said, at last presentable. "How are you feeling?"

Jill offhandedly smiled and responded. "I'm a bit uncomfortable, in the head and stomach." She frowned. "I made a spectacle of myself at the restaurant, didn't I?"

Temple looked hard at her before responding. Jill tried to read meaning in his gaze, and again failed. "Well, I was a bit worried, but when we got back here . . ."

"I don't remember anything past the second drink." This, although true, was misleading. She knew that together they had engaged in sex during the night; she merely didn't remember any of it. Would Temple deny it, assuming her to be unaware that anything had happened beyond his tucking her into bed in a fatherly fashion? Or would he regale her with a tale of how she, in an intoxicated haze, had entertained him hungrily? Indeed, the only possibility that she failed to consider was what had actually happened.

Temple lied; Jill assumed him to be telling the truth, and was reassured. "You were dazed, but seemed . . . um . . . willing, so we . . ." Only the unreadable expression on his face discomfited her.

Temple sidled past Jill and into the kitchen cubicle, where he popped the seal on a self-heating breakfast for two. Setting the small tray on a fold-out table, he dragged two stools around. Jill sat herself to eat.

Temple adroitly pushed a newsmagazine across the table so that Jill could read the headline. "More news about the planetary independence revolutionaries. What do you know about what they're up to?"

"They're just a bunch of silly people," Jill said. Temple could only marvel at her acting ability. "Why do they need to go around arguing with the Concordat?" she continued. "Our independence is guaranteed by the First Charter, or whatever it's called." Dimly remembered lessons from her early schooling came back to her. How long it seemed since she had been an innocent, overly serious teenager, interested in politics, interested in science, interested in boys . . .

"A piece of paper!" Temple sneered. "If the Praesidium wanted to void it, it would, within hours. We're talking about power here, and the revolutionaries think they've got just a little bit more of it than is good for them."

Jill, stung, searched for the right words. "The world's Enabling Charter is a bit more than just 'a piece of paper.' *Your* Praesidium signed it, and *your* Supreme Council of Sectors voted for it. It contains real guarantees—"

"Like what?"

Jill thought it over. She refused to give Temple the pleasure of seeing her sputtering in rage or floundering about in confusion. "What guarantees do you have that you'll be paid next pay period? What guarantee do you have that you won't be arrested and shot someday for no crime at all?"

"The Navy would avenge me. Your revolutionaries know that."

"Is that all it comes down to? Whoever has the most warships—"

"Of which your planet has none."

"No. We have none. Is that all that matters to you? Guns, bombs, soldiers? I like to think that law and order depend on more than ordinary force."

"Don't discount force. With the right equipment, fifty men could poison every person in this city. Two hundred dedicated, well-trained men could disrupt things sufficiently for another, say, five thousand to try for a coup. The revolutionaries, of course, don't have that strong an organization, but I'm sure they think of things like this constantly."

Jill could scarcely credit her senses. Across the table from her, a man who had twice been her lover was talking calmly about atrocities nearly as hideous as the Theury war.

"Why would we want to poison our own world?" she asked, trying for a reasonable tone. Temple gave no sign of the interest that he paid to her exact phrasing.

"The revolution," he said casually, "is, in concept at least, against the Concordat. The killing of innocent bystanders is viewed by the movement's leaders as no more than a sorrowful necessity. Indeed, the very concept of innocent people in an all-out war of this type is not recognized by those leaders."

"That's nonsense. You're talking ancient history." By all the gods that weren't, Jill was *not* going to become angry. "If I didn't know you better, I'd think that this was somehow important to you. Look." She flipped the magazine over. "Ostler's. You can't call that a reputable magazine. You're in the Concordat Navy; certainly there's someone you can talk to who really knows the truth. Or you could ask our ambassador, or . . ."

Temple appeared not to hear her.

"*I* know the truth. These revolutionaries are very dangerous." Temple's expression grew ugly. "The Concordat has no intention of 'taking over' this world, as if we'd do it merely for the sport. On the other hand, the revolutionaries want to extend their control beyond the planet and into space. Your enabling charter prohibits exactly that, so the revolutionaries want to scrap the charter."

"The charter promises that anybody can hold any sort of private opinion he or she may want to," Jill said, still trying for a reasonable attitude. It occurred to her for the first time that she might be afraid of Temple, that if she snapped in response to his rude suggestions, he might actually strike her. Ordinary brutality wasn't unknown to her; some of her customers had been extraordinarily savage. Temple frightened her in a way they hadn't. Lustful rage was understandable, if far from pleasant. She couldn't comprehend Temple at all, however.

"Until they begin to band together and plot crimes."

"When they do that, then they should be arrested and charged with conspiracy." As far as Jill was concerned, that closed the subject.

Temple, perhaps sensing her attitude and knowing that no further information was forthcoming, snatched up the magazine, thumbing through it to the article on the revolutionaries. Jill, hurt, began to gather her things together, preparing to leave.

"Don't go," Temple said over the magazine. "I had some plans for the day."

"I'm not sure I want to be included. I have a job, you know."

Temple snorted. "Sure. Whoring at Lady Titania's."

Jill paled, and her hand clutched at her abdomen as if she had been kicked. A grayness swam at the edges of her vision; a voice she didn't recognize as her own asked plaintively, "How long have you known?"

"A while."

"What do you want?"

"Only information. Please sit down." To her, his suddenly careful and considerate attitude, delivered through a lopsided leer, was not the mockery he intended, but was grotesque, unnatural, bizarre. Then he stood, a menacing shadow in her blurred sight, and pulled a stool close for her to sit upon.

Jill took his proffered wineglass but, afraid to drink it, she merely pretended to sip.

"I know all there is to know about you," Temple lied. "I know your clients and what they pay. I know who your friends are, and your enemies. I know your dreams."

Jill's mind cleared, and slowly her sense of perspective returned. It struck her suddenly that the worst he could do to her was kill her. His power seemed limited, at least in that way.

"There are, of course, things I don't know," Temple continued. "I'll find out, though, one way or another."

"I'd like to leave now," Jill said experimentally.

Temple only smiled. "I'm sure you would. And when you've told me everything I need to know, then you may leave."

Jill sighed. "Ask."

"Who is your immediate superior in the revolutionary party?"

"I'm not in the party."

"The second time you lie to me, I will strike you. The third time . . . won't happen, right?"

"You'll want to think I'm lying, even when I'm not."

Temple considered that, raised his hand, and lowered it. "This is no time for you to be cute or clever. If you truthfully answer my questions, you'll be okay."

"Then ask questions I can answer," Jill snapped. Instantly she regretted it.

"Who is your immediate superior in the revolutionary party?"

Jill said nothing.

"Very well. One more question, and then all bets are off. Who is James Tyler?"

Jill fought to keep her reaction hidden; despite this, or perhaps because of it, a slow, hot flush crept up her face. "He's just a man I met . . . at work . . ."

"I see."

Without warning, the flat of Temple's hand cracked violently across Jill's face. Her head rocked back from the rude blow; for almost a second, full unconsciousness claimed her. As she recovered, the first thing she realized was that he'd sprained her neck. For some reason, though, the pain there and in her face seemed remote and unimportant. Jill tried to stand; Temple casually shoved her back.

"Last chance, slut. Who is he?" When she didn't answer, he grabbed her by the wrists and half-lifted, half-dragged her into the apartment's bathroom, shutting and locking the door. Through the thin panel she heard him explaining what was to happen next.

"I'm going over to the Spaceport to make my report. When I come back, I'll have a full team of trained interrogators with me. They'll take no insolence."

It was a bluff; in truth, Temple didn't dare make a formal arrest. Not yet. He was going down to the corner store to find a bottle of something cold, leaving his unresponsive prisoner to face the terrors of her own charming imagination.

Jill climbed to her feet, touched her sore face, and gazed about the cramped bathroom. The tile floor was slick and damp; the air was humid from their morning showers. She examined her face in the mirror, and gingerly massaged her neck. The door slam startled her, until she realized it was only Temple, leaving. After a few minutes she knew it was no trick; he really had left her alone in his private prison.

No one will take care of me if I don't, Jill knew. *I haven't believed in the "protection of the law" for years. All he has to do is get to the Spaceport with me, and take me away; from there on, the laws of this planet no longer apply. I wonder if kidnapping is against Concordat law?*

I'm not a revolutionary! Never. I keep to myself, because it's safer that way. The revolutionaries are like everyone else—they only care for their own goals. Anyone else can burn, for all that they care.

She turned to the door, trying the opening lever. It didn't yield. Leaping against the door with all her strength, she sought to pry it from its slot. That too failed. She turned to the shower, but it was as she remembered: no window.

She felt her reason begin to tumble. In a frenzy of rage, she hurled herself against the door, which, although thin, gave only slightly and left Jill sprawled on the slick floor.

Her own shriek of rage, frustration, and betrayal startled her, but it cleared her head for the moment. She stared at the door as if it were Temple himself barring her way, Temple standing with his unmoving back toward her. She lifted her foot and, praising herself for her foresight in buying durable, street-worthy shoes, lashed out at the door as she would have at the base of Temple's spine. The sliding door popped loose from its brackets with an unnerving caw of rending plastic and metal.

Jill mopped at her sweaty forehead, fearing for a moment that she would find Temple waiting for her in the apartment's main room. He wasn't there—and a quick search of the apartment turned up no cash or valuables. She wasted no further time in making her escape.

The hallway was clear, and one of the two elevators at the end was halted at this level. She rode it to the main floor, then, in mild panic, pressed the button that would take her on down to the third subbasement. At the main floor, as the door opened, paused, and closed, she held her face down, looking at her sleeve as if at a wristwatch, hoping to avoid notice, in case Temple had posted observers.

I'm being silly. If he had spies, they would have been in the apartment with me.

Even so, when she arrived at the desired level, Jill stepped forth briskly, prepared to run. No one was in sight. She walked up the traffic ramp to the street level, and from there to a moving sidewalk heading south.

Soon, mingling with the hundreds of people out on the streets and sidewalks, rejoicing in the crisp, open morning air and sunshine, she began to review her options. They didn't seem promising.

I can't go to the police. I've been arrested twice for

prostitution—and the police can't be bothered with riff-raff. So what happens when those riffraff need help?

Thirty years ago I could have gone to one of the dozen or so gangs that roamed the crummy areas of town, or to the big gang that they once lived in fear of. Everyone must have been afraid. When they broke the gangs and executed eight out of every ten members, they also made it illegal for more than eight people to be in one place without a permit.

I sure as hell can't go home . . . do I really think of that cheap whorehouse as "home"? When Temple phoned me there, he must have already known who and what I was. Any half-assed computer could have told him the name of the place he called. Why didn't I think of that earlier?

How much danger am I in? Can he and his spies come and take me away? I could go to the revolutionaries . . . except that they'd only think I was spying on them, or that Temple had released me so I'd lead him to them. And that might be true. What the hell do I know of the revolutionaries? They put out a crummy, half-smeared newsletter, complaining of Concordat imperialism. That song's eight hundred years out of tune.

I once knew these streets as friendly. Now every face seems turned toward me, and every eye upon me.

By sheer force of will, she kept herself from whirling about to look behind her. She was more afraid, she decided, of surprising a following man, of meeting his gaze and *knowing*, than of her own imagination. With terrible patience she waited for the moving sidewalk to bear her to its end, within walking distance of the vice district. There, she would be as safe as she could ever be, anywhere.

The day wore on toward midmorning, the golden sun gliding high into the cloud-flecked sky. The deep shadows shrank to dim puddles. Jill carried with her a personal gloom. *It's always bright before the dusk*, she quoted to herself. Where was she to stay this night?

I can't apply for the dole, because I'd have to use my name, and Temple could track me. I have no friends;

*none whatever. Glory and Sylvia might worry about me
when I don't show up, but even if they could do something, they probably wouldn't. One day, I appeared at
the door of Lady Titania's, free for the first time in my
life. The headmistress—so she calls herself—had me
strip. To her, I was a trained animal offering myself for
hire. "Are you healthy? Are you lithe and nimble?" As
if I were applying for a position as a cook or a maid. I
told her that there were perversions I no longer cared to
perform; she glanced sidelong at me, and after a moment agreed.*

*Where am I going to go? I can't even get another job
whoring. They'd want more identification than I can
give. What in hell am I going to do?*

Jill wandered until dark. Necessarily, she avoided
going to anyone she knew; but streetwise, she had to
search for a contact, and for a patron. She spent the
night curled up under an overpass, shivering every
time anyone walked by. No sleep came to her, and she
would not have welcomed it in any case.

During the night she thought again of James Tyler.
She saw him tall, striding over the city like a colossus,
his hair golden in the sunlight. She was mulling over
this image when a slight noise recalled her instantly to
reality. The darkness was as thick as black sailcloth,
and the cold seemed to flow from above in a stream, hug-
ging the ground. At a distance, two voices argued. Even
farther away, she could hear the sounds of the city at
night: traffic and pedestrians, occasional airplanes, even
a rare spaceship being boosted harshly into orbit.

From orbit Tyler had come. That was the way he
would go, perhaps had already gone . . . No. She knew
that he was still on this world, on Theury continent,
involved in whatever struggle had called him, for struggle would always be part of his life.

Why did she love him? Jill had no answer. He in no
way resembled her father . . . and the mere fact that
she had subconsciously been making that comparison
startled her badly. Her father had thrown her out for
the licentious and wanton crime of having been raped;

Tyler had grabbed her for a hot, if innocent, kiss and had then withdrawn in puzzlement, almost as if apologizing. How could she compare the two? Tyler would rescue her, given the chance, not scorn her for her helplessness. He would come to her defense . . .

The reality of her plight struck her again like a blow. *What in hell am I going to do?*

Fulmer Garvey watched attentively as James Tyler spoke into the small radio. The two were sitting on a cool boulder beneath the shade of a small stand of stunted trees. Not far away, the helicopter sat motionless, bright sunlight glinting off its plastic canopy. Garvey half-reclined against a rough and shaggy tree trunk; Tyler lay on his back in a pose of extreme relaxation. Only by watching closely could Garvey see the tension that tautened Tyler's nerves. Even at ease, the hired killer was tight, ready for violent action. His words over the radio were easy, insolent, delivered in a quiet tone. Garvey could see the effort that easy tone cost, only by knowing exactly how to look.

"Grand Admiral de la Noue?" Tyler said, his face showing that he knew full well to whom he spoke. Garvey couldn't hear the response.

"I'm sorry; your authority doesn't extend quite this far." Garvey froze in shock at Tyler's words, and at the cool way he tossed off an answer that could only be mutinous. "As long as you're in the area, look up my travelling orders."

There was a short pause, during which Garvey tried to catch Tyler's eye. Tyler ignored him.

"Wrong," Tyler told de la Noue. "File Black Book, code nineteen. Look it up. And it won't do you any good to try to zero in on this transmission; it's being relayed through an automatic satellite station."

That confirmed Garvey's fears.

"I'd love to stay and talk, but that wouldn't do, would it? Tyler out." Snapping the radio off, he dropped his arm to his side and lay unmoving.

"James?" Garvey asked.

"Yes?"

"Was that what it sounded like?"

Mocking answers fluttered through Tyler's mind: rude assent, sly denial, crude counterassertion. There seemed no point. "Yes."

"What do you intend?"

"Well, to begin with"—Tyler levered himself to a sitting position, and looked about—"this radio can be used as a location detector, so . . ." With that he smashed the hard plastic case against the rock. The case cracked. Two more blows opened it fully. Tyler fiddled for a few minutes with its circuitry. With a quiet smile of triumph, he ground several small components into the stone surface, and turned and pitched the wrecked device into the ravine beneath the boulder.

"What about the helicopter?" Garvey asked.

"We'll have to leave it here, of course. They'll find it in about two hours, I'd guess."

"In that case . . ."

"In that case . . ." we have about two hours to be somewhere else." With a small grunt, Tyler threw himself to his feet, carelessly leaped down from the boulder, and strolled through the high grass to the waiting helicopter. Garvey followed.

At the vehicle, Tyler unshipped his rifle, assembled it, and slung it over his back. Three full clips of ammunition joined the knife at his belt, along with a canteen of protein-based drink. Garvey received a backpack full of survival equipment. As he was handing his partner the firestarter, Tyler hesitated, then switched it on, and ran the barely visible globe of high energy heat through the helicopter's radio. After a few minutes Tyler pulled the firestarter away from the smoldering radio and glanced at it.

"Charge is dead," Tyler said carelessly, and flipped the device over his shoulder. Garvey looked at it lying, spent, on the flattened grass by his feet, and shrugged.

"Shall we be off?"

The day was unusually fine, although the sky was still very slightly dimmed by high atmospheric dust. The weather-breeding heavy particles seemed to have precipitated out; the cool mountain air was nearly perfect for long-distance walking.

As they topped a small rise, the grandeur of the high mountain range was revealed to them: Sharp crags fell away into wooded valleys and bottomless ravines. Above them, the highest mountaintops bore snowcaps. Thin white plumes of waterfalls could be seen glinting in the distance. To the travellers' left, the mountain climbed yet higher, and it was that way they wanted to go. Already they were nearly past the treeline. Before long they would be past the brushline, treading on naked rock.

Tyler unfolded a map, and steadied it against the gentle breeze. Long minutes passed.

"We skirt this face—there's a trail, of sorts—until we come to something called Fifth Summit. That's where we'll pick up his trail."

"How do you know?"

Tyler grinned. "It seems to be the only settled area for five hundred kilometers. If he's anywhere nearby, he'll have to be heading there."

"Maybe he's not headed for a settled area. He might have a cabin somewhere, on a small creek, for instance."

Tyler sighed. "That's a possibility. It's actually the first thing a normal guy would look for. But this guy needs people: he needs lots of them, I think." He looked down again at the map. "Hell if I know what his plans are. But I'll bet that he heads for people. Look here." He held out the map, and sketched with his finger as he spoke. "This high pass is perfect for defense. The one road through could be easily blocked at either end. Further, it drops directly—to the east here—into one of Tertheur's richest farming valleys. It's a real nice lair for a bandit king."

Garvey noted, saying nothing, that the fiction of searching for a missing Concordat ambassador was now forever gone. Would Tyler kill his partner in order to prevent betrayal? Garvey thought not, and hoped he'd correctly judged this ever-anxious assassin.

Petulantly, Tyler folded the map. "Anyway, since it's a road bottleneck, it can't hurt to go there and ask."

Garvey had to agree.

Several hours later they came across an ancient roadway, no more than a flat track carved into the dirt. Overgrown and rutted, it was nevertheless a road. The two men trudged along it with a tireless stride, simultaneously alert and at ease. Gradually, the road sloped downward, following the steep hills to the left.

By the late afternoon they had covered some thirty-five kilometers. Although much of the day's walk had been descending, overall they seemed to have gained a little in altitude. Tyler's map put them at roughly seventeen kilometers from the main road through the high pass named Fifth Summit.

Just past sundown, as they prepared for sleep, a portion of the Concordat fleet passed overhead. They could see a dozen luminous specks and two ships large enough to actually have a visible size. Following these vehicles in their swift east-to-west flight was a monster that Tyler had not expected: the *Fair Phyllis,* looking like a glinting needle in the heavens. Silent and swift, the ship glided majestically past.

In a way, the sight reassured Tyler. He knew those ships to be, in name at least, his allies. They could rescue him from his dangers; they would eventually take him away from this half-dead world. In another way, they were his foes, bristling with eyes to spy upon him. They held cameras that could see the warmth of his body against the chill ground, or, if aimed directly at him, could recognize his upturned face in daylight. Perhaps his insulated sleeping bag protected him from the first doom. He was safe from the second because of the sheer size and grandeur of the mountain range. Only the most unfortunate of chances would catch him exposed at the very moment a camera's field of vision happened to linger upon him. Nevertheless, eyes were upon him, eyes backed by unfriendly intent. He reminded himself to stay close to screening underbrush.

So de la Noue wants me to return. To face arrest. To let myself be executed for crimes of her own authorization. Has it become politically expedient to throw her assassins to the dogs? Perhaps she's under some sort of

*pressure from the Praesidium? Or is it possible that
she's not responsible for the Black Book, that some
other branch instigated it, and that I've been working
all this time for someone else? She certainly didn't
seem familiar with my name, or even with the Black
Book.*

*Maybe one of her underlings set it up—the man who
had me released from prison? I, along with fifteen or
twenty other well-trained, brilliant assassins, am working for de la Noue's interest, but without her knowledge
or consent. Maybe she only recently discovered this,
and all she can feel is betrayal.*

*It makes sense. When Chief of Naval Intelligence
Horst left office in disgrace, he carefully left the details
of the Black Book where they could be found by his
successor, that sap Higgins. Higgins then could either
tell people what he'd found or keep quiet and use it
himself. The man was smart enough to do the latter.
Not bad.*

I wonder what went wrong?

Within minutes the ships had passed below the horizon. Tyler yawned and went to sleep. If, in his dreams,
he visited Jill, he couldn't clearly remember it upon
waking.

Toward noon of the next day they hit the main road.
No one was in sight, a fact that did not reassure Tyler
at all.

"Too many choice ambush sites," he murmured to
Garvey, indicating two or three visible from the road.
"That overhead—or there, where the road curves out
of view."

"The hillsides are too rough for us to go cross-
country," Garvey objected.

Tyler surveyed the terrain to either side of the road.
"You're right, damn it. That's why bandits would choose
this pass. No one can sneak up on them . . . not easily,
anyway, and not in force."

"What do we do?" Even as he asked, Garvey somehow felt he knew the answer.

Tyler looked at him. "We keep going, along the road. What did you think?"

"I'm with you."

"I thought you might be."

Keeping to the center of the road, they moved on— alert, because they knew they could die at any time, without warning. Tyler was very much aware of how great a temptation his rifle offered, and how much a threat. Still, he felt hopeful, trusting to luck and to human nature. Someone had once told him that every animal, every creature of any sort, had a one-word rule of behavior. For the hunting Crayl, circling in the depths, the rule was: "Kill"; for the house-thest, kept as a pet: "Play"; for humanity: "Talk." In this case, it was like a promise of survival: They would be talked to before they were slain. And Tyler could use that to his advantage. Threats, shouted from a covert; a snarled curse; a warning to halt; any of these would warn Tyler, give him an edge.

What he never expected was the blockade set up not far along the road: Concordat Marines.

"Back off the road, Garvey," he hissed. After a minute: "They haven't seen us."

Garvey kept his wits about him and followed Tyler into the drainage ditch on the upper side of the road. He watched with distaste as Tyler pulled his rifle free and took careful aim on the roadblock. He had, a while ago, resigned himself to watching, uncaring, while Tyler murdered anyone and everyone that he cared too. Garvey only hoped that *he* was not on the list. Now, after they had survived this long together, he felt some measure of security. As for the roadblock . . . *I've seen my country die. What do I care for some offworlders?*

But Tyler was only peering through the high-powered scope at the Marines ahead and above. It was a strange relief to Garvey when Tyler lowered the rifle and slung it on his back.

"Too many of 'em," Tyler hissed in disgust. "We'll have to go around."

Garvey looked uphill and downhill. "Steep, rugged terrain. It'll take us all day, at least."

"Best to start now, then," Tyler snapped, heading back along the road. Within half an hour they found a feasible ascent. One at a time, they started up.

The day became quite chilly. The sky grew overcast, until the sun was no more than a moon-bright circle through the whipping clouds. To Tyler and Garvey, clinging like flies to the high cliff-faces, the world shrank to an arm span of stone and sand. Four hours had passed before they arrived at a steeply climbing ledge that looked safe enough to take them above the Marine roadblock. Not half an hour along that path, they ran into high winds, which reduced their advance to a crawl.

"I've never worked so hard . . . for chancy pay . . . in my life," Garvey growled.

"Complain if you want," Tyler snapped. "*I* don't get paid for this at all."

"You're not serious?"

Tyler relented. "I get paid the same amount whether or not I succeed. But the more successful I am, the more often I receive assignments."

"How much farther can we go along this ledge?" Garvey asked, somewhat nervously changing the subject.

"We're almost there. Watch out for that slick rock."

After a long climb, moving crab-wise across the high cliff-faces, they found a steep cleft that shot farther up into the hills. The two climbers rested briefly at the bottom of this knife-slash of a gully. Tyler wrestled with the map as it whipped in the icy wind. Garvey looked up, and was startled by the looming black masses of cloud boiling into sight. He got Tyler's attention and pointed.

"Don't tell me it's going to rain," Tyler growled in frustration.

"Looks like it, sir. I think we'd better get out of this gully, in case of flash floods."

Tyler folded the map, looked up once more, and set a steady pace up the north face of the gully. At the first tentative splatters of oversized raindrops, he steepened the angle of his ascent. Soon the rocks were dangerously slippery, and climbing became more than ever a test of nerves.

The rain began to fall in earnest. Great sheets of water cascaded from the lightless sky. Torrents fell across the rocky uplands. Small rivulets ran in muddy streams down the sheer face of the chasm. To Tyler's relief, there was no display of thunder or lightning, only the hammering of the falling water. He and Garvey were soon wet to the skin.

Two hours later, as they topped one set of rises and cautiously climbed to their feet, the rain slowed and ceased. For a moment the sun showed itself below the clouds on the distant western horizon; then night fell.

The silence of the hilltop was broken only by the distant chatter of running water in the many gulleys.

"This world," Garvey whispered, "has been frightening ever since the war. I've never seen it rain like that."

"It was quite a storm," Tyler agreed, brushing his wet hair back from his forehead.

"It was more than just the storm. It was . . . everything, all at once. We thought we had this world tamed, and . . ."

Tyler sensed, dimly, his partner's awe, but the assassin felt only damp.

"Mountains are always weatherbreeders," he said finally, regretting that he had to sound so disappointingly rational. There was indeed something awe-inspiring and elemental about a storm that heavy, something great and soul-shaking. Tyler wasn't immune to the feelings, but refused to surrender himself to them.

He stretched out and wrapped himself in his sleeping bag. Nearby, Garvey accommodated himself likewise. The two did not speak. Heavy darkness cloaked them from each other. The rushing of the streams made a soothing background clamor.

Beneath James Tyler, the hard ground pressed upward, supporting him in his fatigue. The noise of the streams wove through his tired mind and lonely soul.

That endless night he saw a sight, all in his sleep.

The dream began in the middle, leaving a false memory—a dream past—as an unrecognized assumption. For years, it seemed, he had been living happily with the young prostitute that he'd kissed impulsively back in Exonidas city. Love had blossomed between them, deep and eternal. In the dream, her face was always near his; her fresh wit had provided the balm that his tired hatred needed, needed with an unrealized desperation. Her smile was the key to his relief, her charm the means to his release. Half of an eternity they seemed to have been together, long lifetimes of joy. She had been a prostitute; Tyler didn't care. He had been a killer; she loved him anyway. Together, as two halves of a whole and healthy mind, they were each the cure to the other's ills.

The dream shifted. Tyler's dream self, in a room dark and close, received from a leering deliveryman a package—a large, flat parcel, decoratively wrapped. He opened it and saw the remnants of his lover: her feet, her hands, her breasts, her eyes . . . The rudely severed parts looked so pathetic, so unalive, sitting in bloodless lumps on the bottom of the box. No doubt could exist. She was dead.

Uneasily, the dream shifted again. Tyler's mind shied from the enormity of his rage as he wreaked a revenge so terrible—so extravagant—so inhuman that even a sleeping midbrain can only sketch its outlines. A warehouse was filled with his victims, the floor awash a meter deep with hot blood. Dream blood, dream corpses, dream revenge. And despite this all, his dream lover was dead and gone, unrecoverable. His revenge had gained him nothing, not even satisfaction. He tried to remember everything about her: her face, her voice, all that he had known of her. All that he could recall was that he had been happy with her.

His dream self raised its heavy pistol, feeling the massive weight of it. His dream self placed the black eye of the muzzle at an angle against his forehead . . . and did not fire. That, more than anything, came as a total surprise to him.

James Tyler opened his eyes to the half-light of the false dawn. The streams still rushed in the canyons; the wind still whispered across the bare hilltop. Far away, the hunting bark of a starving wild animal echoed in hollow loneliness against the bare crags. Beside him Garvey still slept, eyes closed tightly against the cold.

Silently Tyler rose and dressed. Sleep was out of the question so, with nothing better to do, he wandered around the boulder-strewn hilltop, gazing across the gullies and the endless upland crags. In the dimness Tyler could see only the silhouettes of the surrounding mountains. Tyler found himself imagining goblin faces in the crags, and the visages of long-forgotten demons, sharp features toward the sky.

The hunting animal gave a last yip and fell silent; the ice-chill skirled past Tyler's ears as he strolled. Almost with surprise he found himself resting his hand negligently upon the grip of his fighting pistol in its trim holster at his right hip. It had saved his life . . . how many times? How many people had he killed with it? He couldn't remember.

Back at the camp, Tyler picked up the two halves of the heavy rifle, and carried them to a sheltered spot out of Garvey's earshot. The rifle had figured heavily in the dream—but as a club, not a gun. Tyler had to admit that the thing was well-enough balanced to serve that way. The heavy chainplastic stock was thick and sturdy enough to . . . to do the things suggested in the dream.

Tyler took a deep breath.

The average assassin survives one-and-one-fifth missions; I've survived a couple of dozen. When a man starts thinking these thoughts, it's time to retire. This will probably be my last mission. When Empellimin is dead, I'll manage to disappear, to avoid the court-martial that the Grand Admiral has waiting for me.

Empellimin. How can I not hate him? He's all that stands between me and freedom. Killing him will be more than a duty discharged, more than a boon to my employers; it will be a relief.

So let's go get it the hell over with.

With that, he spun on his heel and went back to wake Garvey. Tyler gave him just enough time to get dressed and ready before stalking into the early morning gloom.

Fifth Summit was nestled in a windy, saddle-shaped pass between two higher ranges of mountains. As Tyler and Gravey eased toward the edge of the town, they noted that the Marine security detachment was following a routine watch. They seemed neither particularly alert nor observant.

The town seemed no more than an outpost of some five buildings—but the charred remnants of three more, and bullet holes in those still standing indicated action here, before the Marines had arrived to restore order.

Sifting through the wreckage were fifteen men, plainly prisoners under the alert eye of a Marine officer. They were probably the survivors of the no-longer-powerful bandit troupe that had hit the area. Five other Marines lounged about, having nothing really constructive to offer the townfolk—all twenty of them—who knew better than the offworlders exactly what repairs were needed.

Edging in from the tumbled boulders, Tyler and Garvey found a good vantage point overlooking the activities of the Marine garrison. The weary day dragged on, the two men taking turns watching, taking crabbed notes, learning all there was to know about the daily routine.

"Their leader, the Sergeant, doesn't seem too security-conscious," Tyler said, toward sundown. He gingerly stretched his cramped legs, taking care that nothing of him could be seen from the town.

"Well, he's got that roadblock to make things safe,"

Garvey put in. "There's probably another one down the other road, also."

"I'm sure of it."

"Why are we wasting our time here?"

"I need to know if Empellimin came this way. If he did, as I suspect, then the delay won't matter . . . if he's on foot. All other cases mean he'll have gotten away, and the whole trip's been wasted."

"But you think everything's okay?"

Tyler answered without taking his eyes from the camp below. "No. There's too damned much that can have gone wrong. He may have taken a side track, although I don't think so. More likely, the Marines stopped him, discovered who he was, and took him back to the Grand Admiral. By now, she might know that it's him I'm after.

"Or he might have a riding animal, a helicopter, or an air car, and we'll never get him. Other things can have happened. He might have been killed in the raid here, however long ago it was. He might even be indoors right now, wounded but recovering."

"All right," Garvey agreed. "What do we do?"

Tyler's answer electrified him. "Tonight we sneak in and kidnap somebody."

"Not one of the soldiers?!"

Tyler turned him a mild gaze of reproof. "Whom better?"

"They'll have sentries posted . . ."

"A sentry, Garvey. One. He's the guy we nab. They won't even know he's gone for some four hours."

"Can we do it quietly? No noise whatever?"

"Child's play." With that, Tyler dismissed the subject, and relaxed against a boulder, sipping contemplatively from his canteen.

By the time it was fully dark, his old instincts and mind-set were back. If he'd been able to step back and compare himself with himself, it would have been with a sad awareness that he recognized his old self, a grinning maniac who lived to slay. Garvey watched, as the light failed, seeing his employer's face settling

into a mask of old hatreds. The color left the world
with the fading glow of the sunset, and all about,
nothing was to be seen but the muted grays of the
lifeless stones.

"Now," Tyler whispered, and set out at a lope through
the field of boulders. Garvey had no choice but to
follow.

The Marine section guarding this pass was not from
a first-line battalion; the sentry standing watch was
little more than a youth, probably on his first assignment. Tyler realized this, and knew the boy to be
helpless against him.

A shape amid shadows, the assassin stalked the
sentry. As the youthful soldier came to the end of his
round, he breathed out, glanced around, and turned on
his heel to return. Something stood before him, its face
inches from him. For long moments nothing happened,
with the sentry frozen in near-shock, and Tyler standing motionless at the boy's front, eyeing him. The
sentry twitched, obviously beginning to think about
shouting or fleeing. Tyler reached up, and, without
effort, pulled off his victim's helmet.

"What . . . ?" the soldier began, and filled his lungs to
shout. Tyler's knotted fist landed savagely upon the
inexperienced sentry's temple. He caught the sagging
form before the combat rifle could clatter to the
ground.

"Follow me," he said to Garvey, who approached
warily. Together they bore the limp sentry away, up
into the bleak hills.

Two hours later, in a well-sheltered hollow, Tyler
deposited his burden onto the cold earth, steadying the
staggering Garvey with his other hand.

"Sorry," Garvey gasped. "I'm not used to such a
pace."

"It made sense to put some distance between us and
that camp. Go rest."

"I think I'd better not. I'll watch . . ."

"While I torture the prisoner? You think you might
be able to talk me out of permanently maiming him?

You're afraid I might be a bit more savage than you'd like?"

"It's only . . . He's no more than a recruit, James. I don't want you to ruin him."

Tyler lit a small electrical lamp, hardly more than a belt flash, and set it on the rough floor of their undercut semi-cave. In its harsh illumination he met Garvey's eyes. Garvey was taken aback by the cruelty he saw in Tyler's face; nevertheless, he stood his ground.

"I . . . don't like torture. I'd hoped . . ."

Tyler waited. When Garvey said nothing further, he let his mask sag into a sad smile.

"I don't like it either. So, we'll try other things, first."

A moment longer they gazed at each other, then Tyler turned about and prodded the captive awake.

"What? Where am I?" asked the sentry groggily.

"You're in a cave, in the middle of nowhere. Nobody can hear you. If I kill you, nobody will ever find you. I need to know some things."

The youth looked up at him in distress. "I can't tell you anything."

Tyler laughed then, a sound that Garvey found terrifying. "Do you know who I am?"

The sentry shook his head. Tyler moved the lamp around so that his face was better lit.

"You're the man . . . that we have arrest orders for," the sentry finally said. "How did you get here?"

"By killing every man in your half-assed roadblock," Tyler lied. "It wasn't very hard."

The young soldier cracked. "What do you want to know?"

Tyler held up the photograph. "Did this man come through your camp?"

After studying it, the soldier nodded. Seeing that his captor wanted more than mere assent, he gulped and explained. "He was picked up by the south roadblock two days ago, and questioned. He met the description of a guy—Potok Empellimin, I think was the name—that we were supposed to keep from going anywhere. But he wasn't the same man."

"But this is his photograph?"

The sentry squinted, trying for a better look. "He was dressed differently, and the guy we stopped was more tanned, but that's the same guy."

"Then the joke's on you. This is Potok Empellimin. Keep going with your story. Which way did he leave?"

"There's only the one other road out of here: the north. He took that. He was with a woman and some kids. He seemed to want to get into Tertheur."

"What was he like? Was he frightened? Guilty? What?"

"He snarled at us, called us names, like 'Green-flag tyrants,' and worse."

"Anything important get said?"

"Just cursing. As if the war had been our fault. Look—"

"Shut up." The reprimand was calm, matter-of-fact. "Did he have a vehicle?"

"He had two big sledges, pulled by dray beasts. The kids were riding. He and the woman were leading. They scarred up the roadway pretty bad."

"How fast could they travel?"

"No better than twenty kilometers a day."

"Did he say where he was heading?"

"He talked about a 'fresh start' down in Tertheur."

"Good. That's what I'm here to prevent." He thought. "Garvey, bring the small pack."

In a moment Garvey handed him the pack, from which Tyler slipped a pair of padded handcuffs and a length of rope.

"What are you going to do to me?" nervously asked the sentry.

"You'll see," Tyler answered cheerfully.

"James . . ." Garvey began, only to subside as he saw what Tyler intended. By knotting one end of the rope securely to the captive's ankle, running it around two boulders—each far too large for any one man to move—and looping it back again to the empty bracelet of the handcuffs, the other half of which was secured to the sentry's wrist, the youth had been pinioned in total helplessness and yet free from real discomfort. The padded metal of the handcuffs kept his wrist from being chafed, and kept the knots of the rope out of his reach; stretched as he was, the noose around his ankle was likewise beyond arm's length.

"I've been wanting to try that one for years now," Tyler chuckled. "But until now, I never had the right conditions." To the trussed captive, he gave some reassurance. "If I'd wanted you dead, you would be. This is just temporary." He looked at the setup, and nodded. "By scraping the rope back and forth over these sharp rocks, you'll be able to free yourself in maybe ten or twelve hours. The sooner you start . . ."

Garvey glanced carefully at the mad grin that Tyler sported. Sometime in the past day or two, he'd stopped understanding his employer, and that fact worried him more than anything else had during the entire adventure.

"Shall we go?" Tyler asked with hearty cheer.

"Might as well," Garvey laconically agreed.

The climb past the northern roadblock was a good deal easier than the first ascent had been. Within a day and a half, they were, for the first time in the whole hunt, ahead of Potok Empellimin.

Again the rains had come and gone. During one of the unpredictable flash floods that crashed down the steep gullies, the main highway bridge along the primary road to Tertheur had been destroyed. The need to double back and find a parallel road had cost Potok Empellimin several hours. Approaching on a hunting tangent, Tyler and Garvey spied him and his small party twice, toiling at a distance through the ankle-deep mud of the older road. Through the sighting scope of the high-powered rifle, Tyler got one good look at the man's face; it was indeed his quarry. Sighing in satisfaction, Tyler lowered the gun.

The look he received from Garvey was disturbed and disturbing. In a haunted tone, the bearded man asked, "Why didn't you kill him?"

A pang went through Tyler, that his partner had misunderstood his intentions.

"The range is too far," he explained easily. "I was just getting a look at his face. The best killing is done at under a hundred meters."

"But it was really him?"

"Yes."

Garvey looked about him, at the terrain formed all of cliffs and gullies. They were now some distance below the altitude of Fifth Summit. Straggling patches of stout brush were beginning to reappear, tingeing the hillsides a faint pastel green. The far-off road where Empellimin and his small group labored disappeared beyond a small escarpment to drop into one of many descending valleys that led, eventually, to the flat fields of Tertheur.

"James," Garvey began, trying to keep his voice level, "I've had a good idea of what you were about, even before you told me. If you want . . . need to kill that man"—he jerked his thumb in the direction of the vanished group—"then go ahead. I'll be paid, paid well, if our bargain holds, for the guidance I've given you, and I guess I don't care anymore who dies. But, if it's okay with you, I'm going to wait here. There's no reason I need to watch, is there?"

Tyler smiled easily. "No problem." His smile faded, to be replaced with a thoughtful expression. "Death is never pretty. The ruins that a high-powered sniping rifle leave of a man's head are even less pretty. But what that man did to your planet isn't good to look at either."

The assassin shrugged. "It won't take me more than an hour." With that, he set off, not downslope, but a bit to the right and uphill, in order to gain a vantage over the slower Empellimin.

The area's dry soil had thirstily gulped down the rain water, leaving the path that Tyler chose dry and sandy. To his sides boulders great and small spread out in endless tumbled wastes. Above him, to his right, the main strength of the mountain range reared up:

snow-capped pinnacles, jagged and blue, standing harsh against the pale blue of the cloudless sky.

The weather was ideal. Soft cool breezes whispered among the boulders; the direct heat of the sun was blocked off, perhaps by a high, invisible layer of atmospheric haze. For James Tyler, the slight exertion of the climb was heartening, strengthening him for the job ahead.

The job . . . He refused to think about it. It would be over soon. Then freedom would come, for a time.

As he climbed, the boulders became greater, until it was easier to leap from one to the next than to pick out a path between them. This rough, athletic mode of going soon had Tyler's face flushed, his heart hammering; he felt better than he had in weeks.

From good footing, a twisting leap threw him through space with all the precision of a champion gymnast, his rifle held out from his body as a balancing weight. The arc ended; he landed on bent knees on the near slope of a still larger rock, his hands scrambling for purchase, his booted feet already moving him up the huge round monolith for his next leap.

Several minutes later, he topped a small ridge and found himself looking down over the road and into the depths of a canyon. Across the wide chasm, another mountain threw itself skyward. Tyler couldn't see the bottom of the canyon; only a sliding scour of rocks that seemed to flow down into the emptiness. Only a moment's inspection dispelled the illusion of motion.

The road was just below Tyler, a thin, nearly level ribbon of muddy ground littered with rocks, shards, and gravel. No one was in sight; Empellimin hadn't yet arrived.

It was a perfect site for an ambush, Tyler judged. A regiment could hide scant meters from the road and never be seen. He found a comfortable position in the shadow of a building-sized boulder, and curled into the smooth, curving, shelflike hollow beneath. His great black rifle extended beyond, in no way visible from the road; his view covered the entire stretch of road from left to right, where it finally descended around a buttress of rock.

First he heard the noise: Empellimin's dray-beasts dragging the huge sledges over the rock-sprinkled mud. A few minutes later they came into sight. Tyler watched coolly.

The paired beasts of burden looked like large, shambling piles of carpet remnants. Strips and tatters of matted hair hung from their shaggy bulks. Harnessed by thongs to the flat-bottomed sledge, they plodded mechanically through the clinging mud.

With them, walking to their far side, was Potok Empellimin. Shirtless, his black trousers gray-patched with mud, his heavy boots rimmed with the sticky stuff, he looked to Tyler more like Benearus, the ancient god of farm and field. The man was in good physical shape, his bare chest deep, his bullet head high on a thick neck. Balding on top, his fierce face showing deep lines, he was nevertheless a craggy example of robust power.

With an oath that was inaudible to Tyler, the lithe fugitive stood still for a moment, letting the dray-beasts plod past him. Leaping the dangling traces of the uphill beast, he crossed between it and the sledge to goad it to greater exertion. Honking plaintively, the shaggy monster complied.

The never-ceasing toil went on, Empellimin urging the beasts onward, meter by meter. Tyler, from his covert, nodded once sadly to himself. The difference between a lively man and a wind-cooled corpse was a trifling thing. In his hands he held the means to the difference. Life and death.

The old religions had the answer. They held that a detachable portion of a man imparted life to the unfeeling soil that was the body. When a man died, the gods debated upon the fate of that portion, with gentle Diezette pleading for mercy and Horor the Finisher demanding punishment. Kretosa judged . . .

Well, the gods are dead. Rightly so. And Potok Empellimin has already been judged.

Around the upper bend of the trail another sledge made its way, dragged by two more beasts, nearly identical to the first two. While Empellimin's sledge was piled high with bales and bundles, supplies and well-wrapped provisions, the following mud-caked sledge was being ridden by a tall, wind-blown woman and— Tyler counted—one, two, three . . . eleven children.

Beyond fright, beyond any sense of adventure, it was plain that to these children the journey was a mindless wandering from nowhere to nowhere. Although they gripped stay-ropes firmly, none seemed at all animated. There was no speech, no song, not even a glance to be given for the scenery of unimaginable savagery and beauty.

After a time, the woman halted her sledge just behind Empellimin's, which he had allowed to stop. Empellimin, who had been watching her approach, stood still, his hands on his hips, a grim smile of approval playing over his lips. The woman approached him, and put her arms around him. Only then did the thick man put aside his stoic manner; he returned her hug with heavy passion.

Disengaging, he stalked uphill to the children's sledge, and boosted each of them down from the high stacked top of it. Each of them received a hug, which they returned desperately.

They're all too near the same age to be related, thought Tyler. As he looked, the familial and racial differences between them grew more pronounced. *Orphans all,* he knew. *I wonder what Empellimin is doing with them. Starting a foundling home?* That made as little sense as any of the other thoughts that came to his suddenly numb brain.

This man murdered over half of this world! What right has he to share in its eventual rebuilding? He's a threat to what I believe in, and I've been ordered to kill him.

He aimed the rifle at a point just below Empellimin's thick neck, tracking the man as he moved. Back at the side of his partner, Empellimin took the woman's hands

in one of his and waved expansively at the bottomless
gully and the rising mountains. She followed his gaze.
For a long minute they stood watching, looking with
their minds at some shared dream.

Tyler's entire being seemed concentrated in his right-
hand trigger-finger. His right eye was pressed hard to
the eyepiece of the combat rifle's telescopic sight.
Empellimin's corded neck was thick and bronzed, an
affront to Tyler's eye. The man's life hung upon the
slightest twitch of Tyler's finger.

The woman spun, and pulled Empellimin to her for
another kiss. Tyler watched. The cold sand of the rock
upon which he lay grated beneath him. The aromatic
scent of the few stunted bushes came to him on the
slow-moving air.

Empellimin and the woman finished nuzzling one
another; with a grunt, he stretched and gestured her
back to the sledge. She complied, walking away without looking back. The children mounted.

Protesting, the dray-beasts allowed themselves to be
goaded into lumbering motion, lurchingly hauling the
great, flat-bottomed sledges down the slope of the trail.

Fifteen minutes later they were gone around the
lower bend, and only the churned mud of the old road
remained to show their passage.

Tyler had never fired.

Numb, his side stiff where he had lain too long
against the cool, smooth rock, he staggered to his feet.
His mind was empty, his head light. Stolidly, with
none of the leaping enthusiasm that had brought him
this far, he trudged uphill, between the rocks that
towered over him. White sand gritted beneath his boots,
and small rocks shifted unsteadily as he put his weight
upon them. It was farther than he remembered to the
site where Garvey waited for him.

Garvey, looking up, saw his employer approaching,
his face an unreadable mask. He waited, seated upon
a boulder, as Tyler neared.

Tyler pushed past him, and dropped onto a seat of
his own. His rifle seemed to slip from his clutching

hand; his two pistols were no more than an extra weight to him. *I don't want to think about it, but someday I'll have to. What in hell am I going to do?*

Garvey handed him a water canteen. Tyler took it and drank. Fearing this silence more than he feared Tyler's wrath, Garvey nerved himself to ask, "How did it go?"

Tyler looked up, but not at Garvey. In the direction of the horizon, he muttered, "Oh, he's dead." *I wish I were. I wish* . . . He drank again from the canteen, and it tasted like cool sand.

The pair of weary adventurers arrived back at the north roadblock within three hours. Tyler's surrender was brief, if characteristic.

Climbing back up the main road toward the small village, the two saw the roadblock, and were simultaneously seen by the men manning it.

"All right, you cretinous replacement depot rejects, listen up!" Tyler shouted at them, ignoring their aimed and ready weapons, taking the attitude of a superior officer. "I've got a big-name prisoner for you. Help me bring him in, and you'll all get pay bonuses. Understand?!"

The soldiers nodded, and their corporal, glancing at Garvey, asked, "Who is the prisoner?"

"What have you got, *krat* for brains?!" Tyler snarled. Then, mock-coyly, "He's me."

"I beg your—"

"I'm trying to surrender, musclehead. Haven't you a warrant out for the arrest of James Tyler?"

"Yes, but—"

"But what? I'm him. He's me. Make your arrest, or do I need to do it for you?"

"Hand over your gun," the Corporal finally said.

"About time."

"Are you really James Tyler?"

"Take me in and find out, dunce."

Thirty minutes later he and Garvey were well in captivity in the makeshift jail of Fifth Summit. A brief interview with the sergeant in command cleared up a few points of confusion, such as why he had been caught going south, when he had last been seen already to the south of the paired roadblocks, and what had happened to the sentry missing for two days.

"He didn't report back in?" Tyler asked, a sick feeling in his stomach, which he in no way showed.

"No. What did you do to him?"

Tyler explained. A detail was told to search the rocks in the indicated area. Several hours later the report came back: Although dehydrated, the sentry was well and unharmed, having failed to scrape apart the rope that bound him.

Tyler asked Garvey, "Would you have had any trouble wearing that rope thin enough to break?"

Garvey shrugged. "Probably not."

The sentry, giving his report in the divided room where the two prisoners were kept, explained how he had managed to get the rope wedged tight between two rocks, preventing him from scraping it in two. His discomfort was not relieved when Tyler's sardonic chuckles of amusement punctuated his report.

Garvey watched Tyler tightly. The trim assassin was displaying a fey, antic mood, a harlequin split in character between rude, vicious jibes and a dazzlingly light humor that found all things inexplicably funny. Like all of Tyler's bright moods, this was a cover, which he used to shield himself from his true, deeper savagery, his black, underlying depression. Garvey, though, knew that something was tearing at Tyler, something that Tyler dared not let himself acknowledge.

"Jailer!" Tyler chirruped. "A crust! A tin of dingy water!"

The sergeant commanding the small outpost sauntered closer to the rude partition holding his prisoners, eyeing the chains that held them tethered. He ran his gaze over Tyler, unsure of what the man had in mind.

"Yeah," he said at last. "Hold on." He tossed Tyler a canteen and a package of field rations. Turning to Garvey, he asked, "You care for any?"

Tyler stood, interrupting Garvey's answer. Although he was held helpless by the chain, he still put on a frightening enough aspect to cause the sergeant to step back swiftly.

"This *krat* is not fit for intestinal bacteria!" Then, brightly: "Is that why you and your men are so fond of it?" Forestalling response, he asked in an exaggeratedly tired voice, "And when are we to be taken from your hands and given to the gentle inquisition?"

"We're shipping you across the ocean to Horla as soon as the shuttle gets here."

"Who is to be my inquisitor?"

The sergeant shrugged. "I don't know."

"You're not good for much, are you?"

"I'm not in chains," came the cruel answer; with that the sergeant let himself out.

His audience gone, Tyler's mood fell from him like a cloak, leaving only the tired, lonely face that was his final mask between himself and the world. Wordlessly, he handed the canteen and strip of ration-wafers to Garvey. Garvey, feeling somewhat sick, took them and set them aside.

After a time, Tyler spoke. To Garvey it seemed impossible that anyone could live with a mind, a soul so wrapped in pain, loathing for self, and utter hopelessness as Tyler showed, in his voice, his expression, his attitude. Leaning against the rough wall of the cabin, letting it hold him up, his feet were braced wide upon the floor, his hands drooping at his side. Garvey couldn't meet his gaze.

"It's going to be bad," he finally said to the intently listening Garvey. "Up until now, as far as the Navy was concerned, the left hand didn't know what the right was up to, and that left me free to act. We were covered. Now that the Grand Admiral is aware of me, I'm as good as dead. At one time, I occupied a cell in her best prison, awaiting death. Someone else thought I was too useful a tool to be thrown away, and so I was spared. The Grand Admiral would be very happy to see me to my execution."

He sighed, and continued. "You'll be spared, and released. Don't worry about that. It may even be possible for you to get the reward I promised you: the fusion generator for Camp Epsilon. Maybe."

"Mr. Tyler . . ." Garvey tried to speak.

"But who the hell am I to be making promises," Tyler snapped, and absolute viciousness undercut his voice. "I belong . . . I belong . . ." *Where do I belong?* he asked, his voice small in the hollow privacy of his mind. *The junkyard of history, with all the other failures? I'm no better than a . . .* Words failed him; misery took a blinding hold.

"Mr. Tyler." Garvey's voice came to him as if from a distance.

"Yes?" he answered, without opening his eyes.

Garvey fumbled for words. Finally, "Try to be okay, will you?" was all he could find to say.

"I'll manage."

Tyler slept during most of the shuttle flight across the wide Sea of Lamps from Theury continent to Horla continent, to the great spaceport at Exonidas city. His cares and concerns fell from him at last, leaving him for a long, rare four hours more free than he could ever remember being. Not even handcuffs could fetter the freedom he felt. He dozed in his seat, his hands crossed on his chest, his face at peace.

Some of this feeling of being at ease stayed with him after he woke. The shuttle had landed, and was being towed to a docking bay in the vast maze of warehouses and hangars behind the boost-grid. A glare of lights came through the grimy windows of the shuttle; Tyler gazed blankly at the lights as they rolled past. He looked beyond them at the endless expanse of the boost-grid, where the deep-set, tungsten-steel rails made a pleasant pattern of reflected light. For a moment the spaceport terminal building was visible through a gap between two monolithic warehouses. Floodlit, its thousand windows blazing, the five-story structure was artistically integrated with the planting around it, dark lawns and tall trees rolling over man-made hillocks.

Not even that sight could stir James Tyler from his apathetic lassitude. Even knowing that somewhere within that building's many ways he would be questioned, worked over, and finally executed, failed to bring him from his drowse. *Not a hell of a lot to be excited about,* he thought; *not really.*

Without resistance he let himself be led across a windswept concrete expanse to a waiting car. Two men in Navy uniforms, Support branch, eased him into the back. The handcuffs behind him were uncomfortable, nothing worse.

Only minutes later the vehicle stopped, and three more men took custody of the prisoner. He was taken out again into the chill, starless night, where the breeze folded his jacket-sleeves against his arms and tangled his hair, and through a door, into an endless corridor illumined with overhead fluorescents. Not many people were in evidence; the sudden warmth tugged at Tyler's already flagging consciousness.

Then he was in a cell, a mattress beneath him, his arms free, and nothing, anywhere, mattered.

Fourteen hours later he awoke. Nothing bound his arms, although he couldn't remember for a moment when the handcuffs had been removed. Gray light seeped through a high, grilled window in the small cell: the cool light of fog-filtered day. He yawned, decided that it helped, and blinked himself into full awareness.

I think . . . I need a change of clothes. Someone in charge had evidently felt the same way, for as he turned about, he discovered, by the carefully secured door, a small package that he delightedly found to contain fresh clothing and several disposable soaped and dampened wash-sponges. The accumulated grime of the past several days came loose swiftly, leaving him cool and clean for the first time since the long hunt began. He gave a nod of thanks to the unknown prison director for the dignity of that bath, and dressed himself in the uniform. That provided the second pleasant surprise of the morning: it was a duty uniform for his rank of Navy Commander, Support branch. Apparently he hadn't already been cashiered.

I wonder what that's going to mean? At that point, he felt too fine to really care.

A discreet minute after he was fully dressed, a rattle at the door heralded a warder. Tyler stepped back as the door swung outward. The pair of guards who stood just outside watched him warily, but without concern. He felt a brief temptation to show them that, by the gods, he was a man to be feared. Putting it aside, he exited the cell and walked in the direction they indicated.

The hallways, while not crowded, were not deserted. Tyler, slightly in advance of his escort, saw in his mind several opportunities for escape. He could have grabbed that passing woman and thrown her into his two guards, tumbling them all in a confused pile . . . He could have snatched that weapon from the holster of a passing officer . . . He looked again. Not everyone in the long hallway was armed, but those who were carried stun-pistols. On impulse, Tyler glanced up at the strips of fluorescents that coolly lit the hall. Visible through the frosted glass cover plate was the distorted image of the stubby black snout of a wide-area stun-projector.

Inwardly, Tyler had to laugh. He'd been a field man for so long, he'd lost touch with station operations. With a ghost of a smile, he gave up his fantasies of escape and walked stiffly, smartly, his private amusement in no way showing, to the bank of elevators on the right.

One of the guards stepped briskly forward to tap an elevator call button, then faded back. Tyler ignored him with an officious arrogance. He was *innocent*, by heaven; he resented this foolishness!

A minute later, after a brief ascent, Tyler was ushered into a fair-sized office and told to wait. He sat.

The room was square, with only the one door to the hall and a wide window to the outside. Papers littered the gray steel of the desktop and the small table beside it; a trash basket was filled to overflowing. Through the window, Tyler could see the overcast sky, a small section of the boost-grid, and the rising hills of the city beyond.

The door opened, and Richard Temple strode in.

"Well," he said, "so you're James Tyler."

Tyler studied the fellow with unconcern. A Navy Lieutenant Commander, Operations branch. He was good-looking, in a burly sort of way. Tyler couldn't imagine the man to have much in the way of brains. This estimate was reinforced when, after a short silence, he asked again: "Are you James Tyler?"

"Yes. I am."

"I'm Lieutenant Commander Richard Temple." The man wandered around behind the desk and seated himself. "I've been ordered to keep you here until a team of interrogators could be shuttled down from orbit." When this dire pronouncement seemed to have no effect upon his prisoner, he went on. "Until then, though, I don't suppose you'll mind answering a few of *my* questions."

Tyler looked past him, out the window. "Go ahead."

"What do you know of this planet's political situation?"

"Quite a lot. If you'll check my orders on file—"

"I have," Temple snapped. Tyler gazed past him, heedless of the interruption.

"Your mission," Temple continued, "seems to be investigating this world's independent status. Very well. That means you'll have run into those elements of this society that . . . have strong feelings about the matter."

Tyler frowned. "The troublemakers? No more than pamphleteers, rumor-workers . . . annoyances. I've ignored them." *I expressed direct disobedience to the Grand Admiral. This line of questioning . . . isn't what I'd expected.*

Birds, whether native or imported, glided in complex patterns over the warehouses. Tyler watched them.

"We think better of them than that," Temple probed.

"Worse, you mean."

"We feel them to be dangerous."

"You're wrong."

Temple nodded. *He says that to protect them. He doesn't know how closely I've connected him with them.*

A period of silence endured. Tyler gazed imperturbably away, over Temple's right shoulder.

"Have you heard of the Planetary Independence Party?" Temple demanded at last.

Tyler blinked. "Yes." He'd read the name in the situations report before coming to this world. Repeating what he'd read then, he added, "Harmless, eccentric, slightly addled."

"How long have you been a member?" Temple asked harshly.

This man was losing some of his control, Tyler judged; and if so, it was a good thing. Interrogators should have more resilience. "Member? I'm not one."

But Temple had his own methods. "Do you know Jill Imfarland?"

Frowning at the floor, Tyler tried to place the name. Nothing came to him. "Sorry."

Temple, sarcastic now, was edging in for what he thought to be a kill. "Oh, don't you?"

"No."

"I see." He paused, and pulled a document from a desk drawer. "Read this." It was a letter.

James Tyler (it read): c/o Exonidas Spaceport Naval Base.

James. Help me. Help me if you can. I have no other friends to turn to. You met me briefly in Lady Titania's, in one of the poorer sections of the city. I know why you were there, and what you did in the locked cubicle seventeen. Believe me, I have no wish to use this knowledge against you; I will not, no matter what happens. I mention this only to cause you to know that I am no foolish caller of false alarms, no prankster. I need your help, and I will do anything you might ask by way of repayment.

By the time you read this, I will be in hiding. I can be contacted through "pest-Benito," one of the many people scratching out a severe living in the south slums. He will know you by sight, and he can bring you to me. If you cannot help me, at least come to talk to me.

Please hurry.

Jill Imfarland.

Tyler read it twice. His frown deepened. He was aware of his interrogator watching him gloatingly, and ignored this unpleasant distraction. Jill Imfarland.

His mind took him back to his first day on the planet, when he had wandered into the prearranged site to pick up his secret assignment. Lady Titania's. He had taken the key from the headmistress; he had wandered down the hallway, past three charming pros. He'd received his assignment. He'd come quickly out of the cubicle, to be stopped short by the three young women. From his embarrassment at the situation, at having stepped unawares into their midst, he had taken an impulsive course of aggressive audacity. He'd pinched the ear of the triangular-faced blonde, swatted the rear of the long-haired folksingerly redhead, and, moved by what impulse he could not now name, had pulled the third of them to him for ... So that was Jill. Her face swam before him in the room that seemed suddenly darkened. Bright, deep, forever eyes, an almost painfully cute upturned nose, midnight hair ...

"So. Who is she?" Temple's voice brought Tyler back to stark reality no less swiftly and thoroughly than would have a slap to the face. For the first time in the meeting, he met Temple's gaze squarely, and even from the neutral expression upon his face, Temple shied back.

But Tyler had no answer for this pitiful creature. Not now. Not when ... something more important needed examining.

Temple suffered from no such delicacy. "Who is she?"

he asked, his voice dangerous in the darkening room. Outside, the sky was growing black, preparing for a rainstorm. Tyler grinned with the sudden thought that it might be the same storm he and Garvey had waited through, across the sea. Again, Jill's face floated before him.

Temple had run out of patience. Slamming a hand across his intercom, he rasped, "Send in my team of medics."

"Medics?" Tyler asked. "I'm not unwell." Already, though, he knew better.

"You will be," Temple said brutally.

Tyler nodded . . . and stood, and bent, and toppled the desk over on top of his tormentor. Temple shrieked, clawing for the gun that was hidden in one of the drawers. The weight of the heavy desk kept the drawer from opening.

With a smooth economy of motion, Tyler lifted the chair that he'd been sitting upon, and heaved it through the plate glass of the window. Instead of shattering, the large pane popped loose from its mounting and fell away, twisted sideways by the strong wind from outside. The fresh air, strong with the moist scent of new rain, rushed into the room, scattering papers.

Tyler waved once to the struggling Temple, and threw himself out of the empty window-way. The wind took him for a moment, and then the unseen surface below slammed into him, driving his knees into his stomach, his heels into his hips. Following a brief moment of blackness, and a longer moment of mindless pain, he rolled from his side onto his front. Judging from the sharp, stabbing pains from his entire lower half, walking was going to be a trick. Forcing one knee down to support him, he half-rose, only to slip and fall heavily onto the slick, damp grass that he had half-landed upon. His legs were out upon a stretch of hard, pebbled concrete walkway. Apparently, one leg had hit grass, and one had hit the concrete.

He tried again, rising clumsily and managing his first breath since the impact. *Why didn't I look first?*

Was it a bid for suicide? If so . . . it was poorly handled.
No bones were broken. He stood lurchingly, and tried
for a second breath. It came in an uneven gasp. With
nothing better to do, he tried to walk.

No alarms had been raised, and with the oncoming
rain, the outdoors recreational area into which he'd
fallen was deserted. By the time he heard the first
alarm bells, he was limping through an outside doorway from one garden into the next. The rain began,
only a drifting drizzle for the moment. He headed for a
grille gate just ahead and to his left, which opened
easily and led him into an open avenue, paved with
grass, lined on each side with high hedges. At its far
end was a sight that sent a twinge of hope through
him: a similar gate, beyond which were visible several
ground cars. He examined his uniform. Amazingly, it
hadn't been torn in the fall, and the grass-stains didn't
show against the black fabric.

Mere minutes later he found a coin-operated, driverless taxi. As he had suspected, however, his pockets
contained no coins.

No way to break into the mechanism, he knew. *They
make them pretty damned secure. Mug somebody for
spare change? Beg? Walk?* Quickly, however, he found
one of the taxis in the parking lot that still had eight
minutes left on its meter. He clambered in, favoring
his left knee, and spoke clearly: "Go south on Harbor
Drive." The machine, he knew, was clever enough to
follow this order without needing to ask for human
assistance from its supervisor, standing by at the radio-
dispatching central office. By the time the driverless
car had to ask, "Where now?" the eight minutes would
have expired. Smoothly, following the invisible guide
paths broadcast from the spaceport, the car drove itself south.

Almost twenty miles south, the car pulled itself out
of the heavy traffic, with an apologetic, "Please de-
posit further coinage." Tyler sat and waited. The re-
quest was repeated, as the car slipped into a vacant parking space near a waterfront hotel. Tyler stepped out of

the machine, which, sensing itself to be free of any ob-
ligation, waited half a minute, and swung itself back
into traffic, heading north toward the spaceport.

Well, that was easy, Tyler grimaced, rubbing his
shoulder. *Now to find "pest-Benito."*

Tyler walked for several damp, painful hours, while
the rain began to fall in earnest. As the sky grew
black with the oncoming night, he arrived deep within
the south slums. He found a safe place to discard his
uniform cap, and, tearing his rank chips from his
shirt-front, tossed them after. Wearing the somewhat
tattered remains of a duty uniform was not going to
lend him overmuch visibility, he knew; a damp and
wrinkled black shirt was close enough to anonymous
for him.

The wind had died down, and the rain fell vertically,
dripping from the eaves of the small streetfront house
near which he took shelter. The lights of the city
shone warmly, blurred only slightly by the unending
rain. He was soothed by the soft sound of the pattering
drops falling onto the near-empty streets.

He was penniless, unarmed, and on a quest that
was, when he looked at it honestly, foolish. But he was
free, and that made all the difference. He strode out
into the rain, his black boots splashing carelessly
through the pooling water.

He was free, and that was all that mattered.

Richard Temple winced under the weary glare of his
superior, Peter Anthony. Anthony's office was larger
than Temple's wrecked one. Behind the great desk were
the dark rectangles of three windows similar to the
one through which Tyler had leaped. Temple was seated
so that he couldn't avoid looking at these silent re-
minders of his failure. He wrenched his gaze away. To
the left was a tall bookcase, filled with thick volumes
of legal references; to the right was a framed work of
art: a nude, which Temple felt vaguely repelled by. He
breathed deeply.

"Now, Richard, I'm sure it wasn't your fault."

Director Anthony gave Temple a look, and dropped his eyes.

"Two, sir," Temple forced out. "I've lost two prisoners, and maybe I should be retired . . . or . . . demoted . . ."

"Take it easy. It's going to be okay."

"If I'd taken the time to tag that Tyler with a radio-active tracer . . ."

"Then you could be sitting there pretending to yourself that you'd planned it this way." Anthony moved his hands over his desktop, as if searching for a dropped pencil. "But you'd be deluding yourself, you know. Not good. Self-delusion is all very good for . . . well, building confidence. But it'll let you down sooner or later."

When Temple said nothing, Anthony went on. "Let's be honest. You . . . didn't cover all possibilities. No one can, you know. Let's see what we can do about picking up the pieces, eh?"

Temple pulled himself together with an effort, and dragged a sheet of paper from his briefcase. "When he escaped . . . he took an autocab south on Harbor, and it let him out by the Silavon Hotel. That's all we have. His voice is on the tape, telling the machine simply to go south . . ."

"Did he tell it where to stop?"

"No; it ran out of money."

"You've got the master tape from the cab company?" In fact, Anthony was asking these questions primarily in order to get Temple thinking straight again. The man was too good an operative to be wasting time in self-recrimination and misery. Good agents, however, are usually emotional ones. *Keep him thinking about business,* Anthony urged himself.

"Yes. They were very good about handing over the file. I copied it into our machines, and returned the original."

"All right. For my part, I've had no real luck with this 'pest-Benito.' Everybody knows him, but no one knows where he is."

"What is he?" Temple asked. Anthony nodded.

"He seems to be an underground rumor-splicer. He's

the man you go to see if you need to know something. For a price, he'll tell you. He's got a good reputation for being honest, and for straight dealing. He's also very hard to find."

"I should think—"

"Very hard to find. He has more names and I.D. numbers than I like to think about. He's probably a good forger, as well."

"If he's that hard to find—"

"No, our Mr. Tyler won't have any trouble. Benito *wants* to be found by him. He doesn't want to be found by us. What 'pest-Benito' wants doesn't seem to be in our power to deny."

"Well," Temple said after a pause, "there are still some things we can do. You've got the authority to have them ordered. Things like all-points arrest warrants, with photos attached . . . full-time monitoring of autocabs . . . voice-recognition circuits on the phone-network . . ."

"Already taken care of." *But you're thinking along the right tracks. Keep it up.*

Temple flushed. "Okay, then . . . Look, I'll get to work on this. All right?"

"Fine," Anthony agreed, not wishing to put on too much pressure. "First, though, I've tracked down a few things. It seems a message came through my office for our Commander James Tyler. It was double-blind coded, under the Naval Intelligence Branch's operation Black Book. I've already mentioned how difficult it was for me to discover that the man is an assassin. Well, it was even more difficult for me to track this message to its destination. It was delivered to him at cubicle seventeen of Lady Titania's."

"That connects him squarely with the terrorists of the Planetary Independence Party."

"I would agree . . . But, 'terrorists,' Richard? Isn't that somewhat strong?"

"Don't underestimate them, sir. Their resentment of the Concordat knows no bounds."

"Well, all right. Anyway, you'll be in charge of finding those two. Currently, I don't like the way things are shaping up. Good luck."

"Thank you, sir."

Temple let himself out, and strolled down the corridors toward his temporary office—his to use while his permanent office was being repaired. Once there, he began to ponder over any way, any way at all, he could get in touch with "pest-Benito."

When, finally, an idea came to him, he sat motionless, thinking it over. There were no flaws; therefore it would have to work. If this Benito was indeed a rumormonger, selling tidbits of information to the highest bidder, then surely Temple's problems were over. Information on the whereabouts of two fugitives was certainly worth a good deal of money, money that Temple had access to. Amnesty on top of that was not too much to offer.

Temple began setting it up.

Early on the morning of Jill's fifth full day of flight, she found herself utterly without hope. The days had passed slowly, desperately, and she discovered several times that she was indeed being pursued. Her acquaintances in the vice district eyed her sidelong as they told her of police movements, and of illicitly monitored radio traffic. They didn't turn her in, despite the attraction of the growing reward, because to bear the name of an informer was a dangerous thing. Soon, though, the reward would climb above the ill-defined threshold beyond which restraint implied foolishness, not loyalty.

Time was not on her side, but surrender was not within her makeup. She felt her lack of options keenly. She began laying the groundwork for a long siege, in which avenues of escape were vital beyond all other considerations.

And by these endeavors she knew she was only delaying the final capture that would bring her into the hands of Richard Temple. For now she was free, but that was proving to be no better than a mixed blessing. There were places she was welcome, places where the desperate congregated, but she shunned them because of the danger of recognition. She managed to scrape by, and knew it to be no better than scraping. Surely there was someone she could turn to.

Her thoughts kept returning to James Tyler. Well, then, she would get in touch with him despite the risk. This decision, made in desperation and without choice, warmed her.

But how could she contact him? In her mind the cold nights she'd spent kept magnifying themselves into a lifetime; even that, though, was better than a lifetime in prison. And at the spaceport, they would certainly cut open any letters that arrived for Tyler. She needed a way of meeting him, without being found by Temple. She shuddered. Writing a letter seemed to be the most reasonable way.

And in her misery, she remembered tales told in the brothel about how rumor-splicers were sometimes better channels for communication than were telephones. She remembered the name "pest-Benito." She remembered . . .

Hours later, as noontime approached, she found the man she sought. A customer of hers; a man she'd serviced. Would he recall her?

He did.

"Hello, Art."

"Huh? Oh, hello . . ."

"Jill."

Art frowned. "Jill . . . ? Hey, yeah. The little . . . um . . ." He lowered his voice. "The working girl from Lady Titania's. What in hell do you want?"

"I need help."

"I haven't got it. Sorry." He turned to leave; she caught his sleeve.

"Not from you. Just listen."

"Hmm. Okay. Give."

"I need to get in touch with a good rumor man. You once mentioned the name—"

"Hush. I gotcha. Let's get off of the street?"

Five minutes later, in a slightly more private place, they sat side-by-side on the curb and watched the passing traffic.

"Rumor or message?" Art asked.

"Message."

"Okay, you'll want Huja-swift. He can—"

"I want pest-Benito."

"Um. Why?"

"You told me that he can be trusted. It's true, isn't it?"

"Yeah, as far as . . . Yeah, he'll do it."

"Where do I go?"

"You wait here; I'll go." Without another word, he stood and strolled toward the center of the slum district. Dire thoughts chased back and forth through Jill's mind. She hadn't given him any money. Wouldn't he therefore go straight to the police? But no, she realized; he wouldn't. Because she knew his name, and could make things uncomfortable for him. Would he bring back the man he said he would? There was no reason he shouldn't, was there?

Fiercely, Jill ignored these qualms. She wasn't going to surrender. Not now. Not ever.

Soon Art returned, introduced the small man with him as "Pest-Benito himself. I'm going." And with that, he left the two alone.

Benito was a short, slim man, overdressed in several layers of warm clothing. He wore an enormous scarf wrapped about his thin neck, and a huge pair of earmuffs slung over his head. His hair was light brown, and his eyes were worried.

"Ma'am?"

"I need to get in touch with a man."

"And?"

"Well, I don't want to be found by the police."

"Simplicity. Write him a letter—no, don't interrupt. I know what I'm talking about. Write him a letter, telling him to get in touch with me. Makes sense?"

"Yes. But what if the police intercept the letter?"

"Well, but you'll have told me what your fellow looks like . . . Do you know him by sight?"

"Yes." Jill had to smile. "Yes."

"It's as easy as that."

"Where will I wait for him?"

"Oh, I can show you to a safe location."

"As for your payment—"

"Now, don't worry about that. We'll work something out."

"I can't promise you—"

"Never worry." He looked about him. "I think it's going to rain tonight."

"Well . . ."

"Come along. A safe location."

"All right."

Not long after, Benito left her in the empty house that he'd adapted for his private use. Curled nervously on a comfortable couch, she held a steaming mug of coffee to her for warmth, and tried not to show her fear. It was a small house, little more than two rooms in all, with fading walls, a peeling floor, and windows painted a dingy yellow. Once, though, it had been a gardener's house, here between two multistoried near-mansions up in the rolling, many-canyoned hills above the spaceport.

There was electricity here, but no lights; a small, bare heating coil and a box of supplies had provided the coffee. The couch where Jill sat was dusty and poorly upholstered. For her purposes, the place was far from satisfactory. For Benito's, it was ideal.

The day dragged on, slowly easing into a rainy dusk. How much of the plan was a good idea was a question that Jill kept asking herself. How could she know that the letter wouldn't fall into the hands of Richard Temple? Was Benito good enough to avoid him while finding Tyler?

The rain on the roof drummed a pleasant accompaniment to her nervous agony. It went against her every instinct to wait in such a closed-in space, such a perfect trap, as this. The air, damp from the rain, dusty from the ancient room, closed in with the nearly unrelieved darkness to clutch at her, to choke her. She didn't dare leave the relative safety of the couch. The slight blurred noises of traffic on the streets outside came to her as menacing rushings; the strange clickings of the old house were insectlike, frightening.

Later, as the evening grew old, she felt herself start awake from some unremembered slumber. A dizziness gnawed at her, until she recalled her plight. Drawing a deep breath, she pulled her clothes more tightly about her, and resolved to wait, awake, for whatever was to happen next.

Not long after—how long it was, she was never certain—a booted tread steadily announced the approach of someone, someone tall and male and ... A door squealed on rusted hinges. The footsteps neared. A light flared in the hand of a man.

"Glad to find you here," said James Tyler.

Commodore Athalos Steldan sat at ease by the gleaming bulk of the main spaceport computers, his boots propped negligently on top of his briefcase as it sat on the floor. Alone for a few moments, he lost himself in thought.

They had him, and let him get away. By such as these are we served. De la Noue's going to be about as mad as I've ever seen her. Oh well. That's the way of things.

He glanced at the data-screen on the computer console before him, and let his attention wander over the many rows of bright red and white switches set into the steel cabinet housing the machine memory.

He marshalled his thoughts. *To work.*

But before he made the radio connection up to the orbiting Battleship where de la Noue waited for a report, he once again replayed the tapes of his interview with the rescued Potok Empellimin. Following the voices with part of his mind, he kept his place on the form-printed transcript that he held carelessly in one hand.

Steldan: Why did you flee?
Empellimin: Foes of the state! Enemies of—
Steldan: What do you mean?

Empellimin: A new beginning! The children of the rapture! The dawn of a day free from the stars.

Steldan: Tell me—I really want to know—about why you want to be free of the stars.

Empellimin: Green flag . . . uh. Green like . . .

Steldan: Like what?

Empellimin: A fresh start! Burn away the dead wood. Only then . . .

Steldan sighed, and cut the tape short. The transcripts could only hint at the horror of that interview; the tape captured only a shadow of the queer intensity of the man's voice. His gaze had been by turns vicious and frightened; the word "green" affected him like a blow. Fierce dreams of some noble empire to be founded upon the ashes of Theury flowed erratically from the strange man's lips. Although even in utter defeat the man was physically strong, vital, he had sat on the floor, curled in inward-turning misery. For no more than seconds at a time, he would throw a fist at the ceiling in defiance, and then succumb to a lassitude, an uncaring exhaustion, not of the body but of the mind.

After three hours of an interview more stressful and agonizing than any in Steldan's career, he had gathered only a few real facts. The man had been quietly moving toward insanity for months before an accident of fate allowed him to trigger the war. The opportunity had been grasped, and eight billion had died for it.

What did he believe? Steldan had wearily followed the twistings of tortured illogic through the poor, damned official's mutterings, and found there only an old song, an old philosophy: primevalism. The romantic illusion of the noble savage, the nature-worshipping nomad, serving the lands that he is granted the gods' permission to hunt upon: This was the archetype that had taken over Empellimin's view of reality.

By those very gods, long since cast out! The song, the story, had had adherents among all walks of life, on every planet known to the race. The illusion of the tall, lean savage, leaning upon his spear, listening to the nocturnal hill-songs of the hunting pack, as the sleek carnivores track their prey through the far thicket: This was Empellimin's lie. The moon rises, silhouetting the sleepless noble, the king of his primitive domain . . .

It was so twisted a vision, so compelling a lie, that it had believers in every society advanced enough to print books. Guided by it, Potok Empellimin had gathered up nearly a dozen of the most promising children—from his country only, of course—and had prepared to use them as the nucleus of his ideal civilization, his ideal tribe, where even the simplest agriculture would be forbidden, and tool use would be the greatest of evils.

Why had he failed to think of the stars? Did he think that the old treaty that guaranteed planetary independence would prevent Concordat intervention?

From the evils of the less than sane, to the insanities of the high and wise. Admiral Higgins, knowing none of this, had seen in Potok Empellimin nothing more than a threat to some ideal of total unity, and had ordered his assassination.

That hadn't worked out too well, either.

What to do? What to . . .

He reached out and, with one hand, typed in a transmission code on the radio console.

"Concordat Battleship," said a cool voice over the link.

"Steldan for de la Noue."

"One moment."

Time passed, gently. Steldan riffled through the transcripts, not seeing them.

"Commodore?"

"Hello, ma'am. I arrived at Exonidas about twenty minutes ago."

"What news? Have you interviewed our prisoner?"

Steldan always hated this part. "What prisoner? Somehow, he managed to escape."

The silence that came over the transmission link was far more eloquent than anything she might have said immediately. Finally: "Whose fault was it?"

"Lieutenant Commander Richard Temple, Support branch, had him in his office when Tyler made one hell of a break."

"Have you spoken to this Temple yourself?"

"Yes, twice. He thinks he can track Tyler down, soon, through a fairly substantial clue."

There was a pause, during which Steldan assumed de la Noue was using her own computer terminal.

"Richard Temple," she said soon, "is currently assigned to Mr. Peter Anthony of the Horltheur security force."

"A civilian? I haven't spoken to him yet."

"It's through his office that the messages to Tyler were passing. He is now aware of this, but I'd like you to take four or five Marines in and secure his office anyway."

"A bit drastic, wouldn't you say?"

"I trust him; that's not the point. You'll be there to find out how those messages are being passed."

"All right, I'll get right on it." Steldan swung his boots down and prepared to sign off.

"Wait a minute," de la Noue interrupted him. "There's more that you should be aware of."

After a moment, a third voice came onto the link.

"Mr. Steldan?"

"Mr. Secretary." Redmond's voice was impossible to mistake. He seemed more serious now than normally, however.

"Commodore, we—the Grand Admiral and I—have reached a decision. This world needs to be brought into the Concordat for its own protection. I think we have no choice but to abrogate the treaty of independence."

"A serious decision," Steldan said, although he had more than half expected things would turn out exactly in this way.

"Of course," Redmond continued, "we won't do anything rash. We won't start any mass wave of arrests.

But things here have gotten as bad as I intend to let them."

"We'll start setting up an all-planet council," de la Noue put in, "but really, there's not all that much for us to do. We'll supervise disarmament, which is most important."

"The most that the ordinary citizen will be aware of is that his tax load will drop by ninety percent," Redmond said with a nervous ghost of a laugh.

"Do you have any assignment for me?" Steldan asked hopefully.

"Just comb Mr. Anthony's office for . . . well, I don't know what." De la Noue was plainly exhausted. Evidently, the conference with Redmond had covered a lot of territory. "We'll take care of everything else through channels."

"All right." Steldan stretched. "Temple was quite worried about a group called the Planetary Independence Party. He seemed to think that they were in some way connected with Tyler."

"The Party," Redmond said stiffly, "is no more than a two-bit gang of discontented argumentatives. Ignore them. And, since their concerns are for this world only, and Commander Tyler has never had *any* involvement with this world before, I think that this 'connection' he speaks of is entirely mythical. Catch your man, and look for your so-called communication channel. We're in charge up here."

"Yes, sir."

"Good luck, Commodore." This from de la Noue. "I want Tyler caught, but more importantly, I want operation Black Book put out of commission."

"Yes, ma'am."

Thoughtfully, he broke off transmission.

His plans came in three ranges. Soon, he would be involved in the logistics of integrating an entire world smoothly into the vastly larger Concordat. Beyond that, there was the whole of the Black Book to study, its other assassins to learn more of. For now, he needed to grab a section of Marines and search Mr. Anthony's office.

What was de la Noue concerned about? The possibility was there that a message might go through ordering Tyler to have some new target slain, but it didn't seem so likely as to be worth the effort of a search.

With a shrug, he stood and donned his cap. A short walk through the complex corridors of the port brought him to Anthony's door.

"Who is it?" Anthony asked in response to Steldan's knock. Without waiting for an answer, he added, "Come in, whoever you are; I'm not busy."

Steldan entered, doffed his cap, and introduced himself.

"Ah. A Commodore. I'm honored. What can I do for you?" He made no motion to rise from his seat.

"I've been ordered to search your office, in case there's a transponder built into your phone lines." Steldan saw that his host failed to understand. He went on, explaining in more depth. "The assassin James Tyler has been getting his messages through your computers—"

"I know."

"—so I'm here to see just how the messages are arriving."

Anthony frowned. "By regular courier, I'd suppose."

"No." Steldan shook his head and gestured to the bank of phone and intercom equipment on the desk between them. "It's coming directly into your computers through your phone lines—we think. It can't be by regular channels, or we'd be able to backtrace it."

"I knew that the operation was devious . . ." Anthony admitted.

Steldan agreed, but saw no need to admit to this man—who was, after all, only a planetary official—just how devious the Black Book really was. "If I may . . . ?" He gestured again to the phones.

"Go right ahead."

Steldan pulled the nearest phone from its cradle and, after a moment's hesitation, punched a three-digit code.

"Lieutenant Victor? Can I have three Marines and an electronics team sent up to office 14-5? No, no urgency. Five minutes is fine. Thank you."

He rang off and seated himself to wait. The office was quite nicely appointed, although the nude on the wall to the right was in questionable taste . . .

"Am I under arrest?" Anthony asked nervously.

"Good heavens, no," Steldan said, mildly surprised. "As far as we can tell, you are completely uninvolved."

"When you asked for Marines . . ."

"Just a precaution, in case we trigger some sort of alarm or booby trap. We believe that the Black Book contains mechanisms to safeguard its existence and secrecy."

"Do you think it likely that you might set something off?" Anthony's expression was still quite uncertain.

"*I* don't feel it's likely at all. My orders, however, are to take no chances."

"Actually," Steldan continued, "it looks as if your office was used as a conduit, simply because you have access to the computers, and also have regular dealings with the Concordat. The messages come by regular courier, true, but are coded to another office entirely . . . or so it is made to seem. Some secret signal triggers a message relay device here in your office, which sends the assassin's orders to the message spot: in this case, Lady Titania's."

"Why my office? Why not some private company's office?"

"Mainly because regularly scheduled Concordat couriers are the most dependable way of getting the word from there to here, and because your phones tie in to the big computers. But be assured, you're certainly not under arrest."

Anthony hesitated; then, when the door opened suddenly, he started. "Here, now . . ." he began, and stopped.

"Sorry, sir. Corporal Banning, sir, with two electronics specialists." The Marine, with his two technicians and two more Marines to watch the door, was uncertain, awkward. He pursed his lips and stood motionless, then asked, too rapidly, "Where do you want 'em to begin?"

"I'll take care of all that, Corporal. Wait outside."

"Yes, sir."

The specialists, one thin man and one woman, quickly bent and lifted aside the desk, making it easier to get at the wiring for the phone. Working smoothly together, not interfering with one another, they ran tests on each of the wires coming from behind the phone, without actually cutting the wires.

The phone rang.

One of the technicians muttered, "What . . . ? Would one of you get that, please?"

Steldan, being nearest, took the phone automatically, catching it on the third ring.

"Director Anthony's office." His face fell. "What? A dead body? Find out! Damned right you will . . . and better for you if you die first! What? Do you know to whom you speak? Just wait there; we'll be over in moments." He transferred the call to the automatic emergency medical system.

Anthony looked at him. Steldan looked back. The two technicians gazed up from where they knelt.

"What was that?"

Steldan went to the door, and muttered a few words to Corporal Banning. One of the Marines followed him back inside, while Banning and the other dashed off.

"What was that?" Anthony again asked.

"Now . . . *now* you're under arrest." Steldan's face was quite grave.

Thirty minutes later, the technicians found the transponder.

With the coming of night, the lights of the city had come on, shining starlike through the veils of falling rain. James Tyler stood and waited on a street corner at the bottom of a descending court. The silhouettes of the old mansions, secure in their walled gardens, thickly planted about with high trees, bulked almost on top of him as he stood, fighting away impatience. To his right, the bottom of the court gave way down into a steep canyon, into which the rushing stream that was the street emptied. Below him were visible the lights of the distant waterfront and a part of the north fence of the spaceport.

"Wait here," the messenger had said, "and if Benito wants to meet you here, he will."

That had been forty minutes ago. Now, Tyler was soaked to the skin, and a dull, growing anger burned in him. At least, he consoled himself, no one was betraying him to the police; that wouldn't have taken anywhere near this long.

And what the hell was he doing here, standing in the driving rain, waiting to be shown to the woman who had desperately written to him for help? He couldn't make any sense of it. If the city's best underworld rumor engineer was on her side, why did she need him?

He wished for a dry spot to wait in; he wished for a pistol. It occurred to him that this was the first time in years he'd been out, alone, without a weapon.

Perhaps, he admitted, the first ten minutes of waiting were necessary for the messenger to run and fetch this damnable "pest-Benito." And perhaps another five minutes would have been needed for the two to scout around and see that Tyler was indeed alone.

But this is no trap! I'm wet, cold, and miserable, and if nobody shows up in another ten or fifteen minutes, I'm leaving.

Twenty-five minutes later, as he stood in angry indecision, a voice called to him from nearby. "Mr. Tyler?"

Tyler blinked, drew his hand through his sopping hair, and turned slowly. "I am."

"I'm Benito. Come along."

Tyler was mollified to note that Benito, too, was completely soaked.

"Where are we going?"

"It's not far."

Resigned, Tyler followed his guide up the steep street, past the large grillework gates of the rich homes. The pavement was slick, but not treacherous. Overhead street lights made tinsel hazes of the thick-falling raindrops.

"In here." Benito pointed to a small postern gate let into a thick plaster-over-brick wall.

"Thank you." It never occurred to Tyler to offer payment. Benito, who had made his own arrangements with Richard Temple, forebore to ask.

"First door. Do you have a light?"

"No."

Benito clicked his tongue in sympathy, and tossed Tyler a handflash. "You'll need it. No inside lights."

"Thanks."

"Just leave it behind when you're through." With this bit of misdirection, he turned and wandered away on the street, his small form growing less distinct under the streetlights. Considering what he'd been paid by Temple, the flashlight would be no loss at all.

Tyler looked again at the small gate set in the wall. It opened easily for him, showing him a narrow, closed-in avenue between high, unclipped hedges. It seemed almost a tunnel, filled with the hushed drippings of the rain through the innumerable leaves.

He shrugged again, and entered. The branches on either side brushed against him; it quickly became pitch black. Not twenty paces in, he felt a door to his left. He opened it, wincing at the groan of its nearly useless hinges. He snapped on the handflash.

Jill was before him, curled in apprehension on an antique and tattered couch.

"Glad to find you here," he said at last. After a moment in which she did not move, and indeed scarcely breathed, Tyler gently set the flash upon a dust-covered table, half-illuminating the old, old room.

"You came," Jill said, marveling.

"For what it's worth," Tyler agreed, pulling a well-worn chair around and seating himself comfortably upon it. He crossed his booted legs, and brushed his wet hair from his forehead.

Jill began to unbend. "It's worth . . . a great deal."

"I don't know. They're after me just as devotedly as they're after you. I haven't any money . . . no gun . . ."

"But you're *here*," she said intensely. "You know

what the hell to do next." She lowered her face. "I'm up against power that's too big to fight."

Tyler rubbed his eyes. "I've got to admit, they can be awesome when aroused. But there are places that we can hide." Jill began to rally as her long-awaited savior spoke. "At the moment, we have: no money, no equipment, no contacts, and no plan. Nothing to worry about." He smiled. "Plans are the easiest thing in the world to build; given that, what can withstand us?"

"Plans such as . . . ?"

He thought for a moment. "How much timber does this continent produce?"

Jill, without understanding, made a guess. "A fair amount, south of here, in the Nyecrags."

"A mountain range? Perfect. We'll make our way there, walking if need be, and I'll sign on as a lumberjack. On every planet I've yet seen, trees are trees, and lumbercamps are busy, bustling, hard-working places, where questions somehow never get asked."

"What will I do?" Jill asked, half-afraid that he was planning a role of camp whore for her.

Tyler shrugged. "Cook. Radio-dispatching. Or you could pick up a little skill with blowtorch, chisel-saw . . . It'll be your choice."

"My choice . . ." she whispered. If so, it would be for the first time in her life. The memories came to her of childhood outings to the high, wooded meadows of the Nyecrags, mountains of tilted stone, where tenacious vegetation had grasped a foothold. She remembered high, narrow roads over tiered bridges and through seemingly endless tunnels; she remembered the scents of luten and fire-flowering curgloss. She remembered the beauty that she had seen, once, as a child: the sky deep purple with the faintest stars visible directly overhead, even in the midafternoon; the crazily tip-tilted horizon that drew one's eyes always to the right, until by spinning dizzily in place the compelling illusion was forgotten in a tumble of damp grass.

Tyler watched her face gone delightfully blank, and tried to think of some way to ease her return when at

last the tyrant reality forced its way back into her
mind. He had no need.

She focused her eyes upon him and, with a charming glance born of both innocent child and terribly
misused woman, asked him directly, "I, with you, together? We'll do this?"

Why not? What future had he anyway? "Um . . .
Yes."

"What do we need? What are we waiting for?"

Like an awakening thunderclap, the answer to *that*
question came to him instantly. "Nothing! Let's go."

There are some evil surprises that no one can expect, and against which there are no defenses. Ser-
pents strike from deep grass; a hidden cancer, all
unknown, becomes malignant; lightning cascades from
an empty sky.

"Don't move, either of you!" The voice, sharp and
slightly afraid, came with a blazing flood of light.
Behind a nameless man who held a flash, Richard
Temple stood, legs wide-braced, a heavy automatic
pistol disfiguring his extended right hand.

Tyler and Jill exchanged a glance that from each of
them, to each of them, spoke sad, shocked realms of
wisdom.

Their eyes met, and in the glare of the policeman's
lantern, each gave and received what was almost a
vow. At virtually the same instant, each thought, as
he and she looked into one another: *Betrayed!—But
not by you; not by you. If only . . . I love . . .*

That took no more than half of one second. What
happened next took only slightly longer.

Temple's pistol jutted, pointing to a spot midway
between his two recaptured fugitives, aimed at neither, threatening both. He stood five meters distant
from each of them, who sat no more than a meter and
a half apart, helpless.

Tyler rose. Temple began to open his mouth to snarl
some wordless warning. Tyler's far leg came around
and bent, so that he knelt on one knee in a classic
firing posture. Temple moved slightly, shifting his shoul-

ders as if under the gaze of giants. (The light flickered, as the policeman *moved*.) Tyler's right hand . . . did things, and came up, the elbow into the left palm, aiming . . . Aiming a gun that wasn't there.

Temple, already on the knife-edge of preparedness, saw what he expected to see. The pistol bucked in his hand; he held it to its target.

Two shots crashed into James Tyler, and three more. He didn't seem to feel them. All were neatly spaced about the center of his chest. He didn't seem to feel them. They *hurt* him . . . but he didn't seem to feel them.

And Jill, knowing from the first what James Tyler intended, was already moving toward the rear door through which she had entered. The concussion of the shots hurled her on her way. She made it to the street. She threw herself to the left, slipped, regained her feet, ran.

A silence followed in the small room, after the jarring of the shots and the momentary plainsong of their echoes. The policeman moved to right his lantern.

"I think . . ."

"What . . . ? Did you . . ."

". . . I killed him . . ."

". . . get him, sir . . . ?"

". . . I think."

Nobody moved.

"Damn, I hate doing that," Temple said, and for a moment believed it.

"I'll have a look," the policeman mumbled, and moved from behind the overturned table.

"I guess . . . I guess I'd better phone Director Anthony."

"The girl . . ."

"She's well away. Damn her." Temple's rage belatedly rose to choke him. "*Damn* her to everlasting—" But nothing, he knew, was everlasting; nothing. "Damn her." Mechanically, he reloaded the pistol.

"No gun, sir."

"I know. It's too . . . *damned* . . . late."

The policeman fumbled with Tyler's body, trying not to look too closely at the bullet wounds. Temple stalked into the next room—so he wouldn't have to watch—and unclipped his belt radiophone.

"Hello? This is Lieutenant Commander Temple: I had to blow him away. All we've got to show for it is a dead body." He paled. Who *was* this? "Uh . . . I . . . think so. Five bullets . . ." He paled further. It wasn't Director Anthony. It was . . . "Patrolman!" he shouted into the next room. "How . . . Is he dead?"

"No, sir." The voice was muffled. "If we get help quickly enough, we can—" He broke off, turning to what grisly task Temple didn't care to imagine. Emergency medical aid was a skill required of police officers of the country, he knew, but could anyone, with no more than bare hands, hold the life from slipping out of someone wounded—Temple winced against nausea—wounded like that?

Temple took up the phone. "He's alive . . . barely. We'll try to keep him breathing—" The harsh answer stung him. "Dammit, he drew on me! I had no choice. Who the hell are you to—" Again an answer both savage and unexpected. *Do I know to whom I speak? No, I don't!* "Look here—" A final interruption, and he found himself tied into the emergency line that would, in tenths of a second, pinpoint his location and dispatch a fully equipped rescue ambulance. A tone sounded, followed by a recorded voice: "Help is on the way, and will be there in exactly six minutes and thirty seconds. Do not move the victim unless absolutely necessary. Help is on its way, and will be there in exactly six minutes and twenty seconds." And so on.

Temple blinked, hung up, and absorbed himself in the utterly useless speculation on just how good the city's computers had to be to tell him so exactly when help would arrive. An orbital station, watching all traffic, could switch all traffic signals in advance, clearing a lane; monitoring transponders could tell the machine-driver where to turn, how fast to speed . . .

The ugly sounds of Tyler's ragged breathing came in

sickening gusts to Temple's ears; the sharp tang of
neodite and of white powder stank in the air. It was a
scent that was well-known to him from firing-range
practice. Nameless rites were being conducted in the
next room, where blood pooled, where the patrolman
whose name Temple had never bothered to learn struggled, hands red, eyes intense, wrestling with steel-
jacketed death. Temple let his mind flee from that
reality. Orbiting stations . . . Transponders . . .

Will he live? Do I want him to?

The patrolman had no time for such questions. He
had a job to do. Later, he would wash his hands, and
take a drug in order to be able to sleep. It would never
occur to him to blame Temple for not being beside him
to help; some people can take it, some can't.

Jill, her eyesight smeared from her uncontrollably
flowing tears, was caught by Steldan's men within
half an hour.

One week later, Tyler discovered that he had a question to ask. A question certainly. A question. Unable
to remember, suddenly, what the question was, or who
it was that he had intended asking, he gave a small
mental shrug, and, instead, woke up.

His eyes hurt, but that was all right, he decided,
because it meant that there was still light, somewhere.
After a fairly long moment, he managed to focus upon
what looked remarkably like a face. He smiled. It
smiled back.

"Good to have you with us," Steldan said to Tyler.

"Um. Um?"

"One week in a coma. You're going to be fine."

"Wh—" Tyler tried to say. His mouth was thick. It
felt somewhat like the first and only time he'd gotten
drunk. He remembered afresh how little he liked the
feeling.

Steldan watched him, gentle concern showing on his
face.

"Why?" Tyler managed to ask.

"You want to know why we saved you? Why we kept
you alive?"

"Y—yes."

Steldan thought about that. "It was hard work, but always rewarding. It's just the way doctors are, you know. We do it because we have to." His cheerful smile took any implied insult away from the words.

Tyler looked blank for a moment, until he remembered that Steldan was, indeed, once of the Medical branch. He'd switched over to the Intelligence branch sometime before the date when Tyler had been sent to kill him. Had failing then made his living now possible? Tyler gave it up.

Steldan understood his feelings. "Rest now. We'll talk later."

"Right." Was that something to look forward to? *To hell with it,* he decided, and slept.

His treatment continued, progressing from subsequent surgery to restorative surgery to recovery to physical therapy. The weeks flowed into one another smoothly, effortlessly. Whatever damage he'd taken—and it was substantial—was reparable, treatable. His arms, weak at first, slowly regained their vigor; he came to be able to draw deep breaths again, which felt good. The pain-killing doses of Coneamile were reduced, dispensed with. The great, ridged map of scar tissue across his chest was cleared away, by what process he never understood, leaving him with a smooth, bare chestful of healthy, soft pink skin. It itched. Some sun, he was told, would toughen it up. Good as new. Until then, no scratching.

He wondered, and dreamed, and made do. The night in the deserted house in the city's low hills replayed itself again and again in his mind. He really wanted to know ... but he put the questions away until a time when it was safe to ask them.

He was allowed to walk, first with a brace, then without. His dexterity returned. One marvelous, sunny day, he was allowed to run two rounds of the track on the hospital roof. He ran out of wind after the first round, and had to walk the second. That, too, got better.

From the roof, the crinkled valleys of the north end of the city were visible, fading away to the sea. In another direction, a long escarpment could be seen: the south flank of a thickly settled mesa. The sun did indeed toughen and tone his chest, and his back, where some of the surgery had carved it, and where fresh, new artificial skin was peeling away into his own natural skin. That, too, itched. The unaccustomed freedom of walking about shirtless embarrassed him at first, but by the time he was able to wear shirts, he had grown to enjoy the partial nakedness. It took him a little time, he found, to adapt again to shirts.

Every day, for his first three days after awakening, he'd had a short talk with Steldan, stretching out to a three-hour chat on the third day. After that, Steldan managed to return once a week. If this was interrogation, Tyler made the most of it. It certainly didn't feel like interrogation.

He spoke freely of Operation Black Book. Why not? Steldan knew most of it already; a lot of what he knew, Tyler didn't. There was no point in holding back information. The Black Book had been good to him, but now that it was scheduled to be dismantled, he told what little he knew.

"Other assassins? I don't know of any. Double-blind and all."

Throughout, Steldan sat quietly, taking notes into a booklet that Tyler couldn't help noticing was bound in black. The irony amused him, and Steldan got a small laugh as well when it was pointed out.

The conversation soon grew serious. "De la Noue wants you executed for your crimes," Steldan said softly. "I don't."

"I can see her point more readily than I can see yours," Tyler admitted frankly.

Steldan merely nodded. "You've been the instrument of the death penalty too many times to be able to speak against it."

Tyler let it rest. "What will happen to me?"

Looking away, Steldan muttered, "You won't be executed, anyway."

"Good."

A smile. "Again, though: why did you contrive to get yourself shot?"

"It seemed like the thing to do." No more than this would he say. Of Jill Imfarland he had mentioned nothing.

"All right." Steldan stood to leave.

"By the way," Tyler asked, his curiosity overcoming his common sense. "Did you operate on me?"

"No. I'm not a surgeon. I was standing by to assist."

"I think that's the most relieving thing you've said so far."

"Why?"

Tyler struggled for words. "I tried to kill you once. I failed. But I *tried*. The thought of you . . . working on my heart, my lungs . . . That thought *hurt*."

"Do you feel better now?"

"Yes."

"Then I've done my job." With an enigmatic smile, Steldan slipped out.

Day by day he got better. Life returned in its fullness to his limbs; his vitality soared to its normal peak.

Where the hell is Jill? he wondered, and more than wondered. *Did she get away? Is she alive? Did I save her, or doom her? How can I know? How can I find out?*

I think I . . . would care to see her again.

No word came to him of her, and he didn't dare ask.

On a stormy night in late spring, Jill Imfarland was caught, as she wept, by Concordat Marines working under the command of Commodore Steldan. Hysterical, fighting to escape, she was eventually given to him for interrogation. Several times she was reassured that no charges were pending against her; she displayed no relief.

The news that James Tyler, while critically injured, was alive calmed her, but did not ease her nervous fear.

Steldan, despite the many clues hurled at him by Richard Temple, dismissed any connection between Jill, Tyler, and the Planetary Independence Party. Temple was clearly deluded as to the Party's importance.

With no reason to hold her, Steldan had Jill Imfarland released.

She had never mentioned Tyler's name. Tyler had never mentioned hers. Temple's tales of scheming and intrigue were obviously deranged. Commodore Steldan did exactly what he should have done.

He could never have foreseen what his action would bring about.

After the most confusing night she had ever experienced, running from joy, to utter horror, to dull, numbed relief, Jill Imfarland found herself standing alone before the lightless edifice of Lady Titania's. Her clothes were there, and what few personal belongings she had collected. She still had her key. In she went, and up the stairs to her room. Glory and Sylvia were not present; Jill supposed them to be happily asleep in the arms of their customers, somewhere else in the city. That was all very well for them. As of tonight, Jill had quit.

Steldan had given her a twenty-credit note, because she was penniless. That would last her until the banks opened in the morning. As for now . . .

Back on the streets, in the never-ending rain, she walked until she was clearly out of the vice district, and rented a room in an almost-respectable old hotel. Her sleep was uneasy, and the memories of gunshots kept frightening her.

In the morning, she phoned the port hospital.

"What is the condition of James Tyler?"

"I'm sorry," came the answering voice of the clerk after a brief wait; "he's not listed in our files."

"Does that mean he's dead?" Jill asked with an iron voice.

"No, no. We don't have him as a patient. You might check the other hospitals—"

"No. It was yours. The port hospital. I'm sure."

"Well, perhaps it was the military hospital, which is also here by the port."

"Yes. He was military personnel."

"Well, I'll transfer your call, but they don't usually give out names . . ."

The transferred call got her no further information. Everyone was terribly sorry, but no names could be given out over the phone. In person? Yes, except that one needed a pass to be cleared for admittance to the military hospital . . . at least as a visitor.

She phoned for Commodore Steldan. "I'm sorry, but he is off-planet at this time, and we cannot connect you without authorization."

"When will he be back?"

"I don't know, ma'am."

Why hadn't she said something when she was talking to him directly? Fear had ruled her then, not love. Regretfully, she gave up. The phone was going to be no solution.

The rain had ceased at last. In the cool sunshine of the late afternoon—she was amazed that she had spent so many hours on useless phoning—she walked the twenty blocks to the spaceport.

It was as she had been told. No admittance to the military hospital, and no information could be provided. Everyone was helpful, and polite, and apologetic . . . but no news was forthcoming.

What in hell . . . ? But no, she decided, wandering about in miserable indecision was no longer to be her approach to what troubled her. She now knew how to act, and act she did. She wrote letters, both directly to James Tyler and to any officials she could think of. The letters to the officials were returned with polite remarks that no information could be handed out; the letters to James Tyler himself were destroyed. She never knew. He never knew.

Steldan never knew, and it was by a strict interpretation of one of his orders that it happened. His concerns had moved along to bigger things, although if he had known, he would have acted immediately to help.

The weeks went by, and another of Steldan's orders took effect, and again he himself was unaware of one of the implications. The letters addressed to James Tyler began to be returned, unopened, with the legend: "Deceased" stamped across them.

It may be a trick of the Navy, Jill decided. *It has to be.* She stopped writing.

The weeks went by, and expenses mounted, and she discovered that she didn't greatly care.

She went back to work. Welcomed as always at Lady Titania's, she found a place, and devoted herself to gaining what scant pleasure she could from the intimate, uncaring contact. Her form and face were pleasing; her hair was rich and long; she was young, and strong, and agile, and able.

It was a job.

"Died?" The look on Admiral de la Noue's face was incredulous. "I'm surprised."

Steldan sat heavily. "So were we all. I've filed a final report. Would you care to review it?"

"No need. I never expected it, though."

"He had five bullets in him. We might have saved him anyway, but he had a self-destructive drive as bad as any I've ever seen. It manifested itself in his unconscious mind, and that affected the healing process."

In fact it did, just not very badly. I'll lie to her to save his life. He is not to blame for what he did under orders. I won't stand by and have him executed, simply for being a good soldier.

I've communicated with Admiral Higgins. He, too, believes that the Black Book is too valuable to be discarded. He, too, is willing to put the best interests of the Concordat ahead of his own. He will make it seem as if he's cooperating fully with her team of investigators, which I will lead. Because of his helpful attitude, he'll receive no worse than a forced retirement of the second class. His lost retirement benefits will come to him secretly from the Intelligence branch slush fund. And I will take over the custodianship of the Black Book, and keep it functioning . . . for the Concordat, not against it.

Damn it, I've been under the descending blade of the Black Book! I should know how it can be abused. James Tyler had three chances at me; he's alive today because he failed. Alive! A fine joke. He's alive because I've written him off as legally dead. The personnel at the hospital, if it ever even occurs to them to ask, will find out that he "died" after leaving. I've told de la Noue he died in surgery. And I'm not worried. Why would she interview hospital workers? She'd leave that detail to me; medicine is one of my areas of specialty.

The Black Book is mine, to be used when and if I see fit. I hope never to use it; I intend never to use it. It should never be needed. But if it ever is, I'll have it.

"Athalos?"

"Hm? Sorry; I was day dreaming."

"What about?"

"Commander Tyler. A pitiable waste. The Concordat needs people like him. He'd have made a capable pilot, for example."

"I doubt it. He was little better than crazy."

"Well, we would have needed to give him some help . . ."

De la Noue smiled. "That's your philosophy, isn't it? 'No one is beyond help.' "

"It's what I believe. Sometimes, though, people have to be stopped before they can be helped. The one gets in the way of the other."

"That's why we're in the military, and why the military is necessary. We're here to stop things, so that others can do the helping." She looked up at a bulkhead, taking in by implication the entire Battleship. "Nuclear-tipped missiles and heavy beam weapons never did that much to help people, did they?"

"And yet our fleet is here only to help the planet."

Her smile turned sour. "We were a bit late." She

sighed. "But we are here, and the world's independence is now a dead letter."

"That's all taken care of?"

"Yes. Planetary council appointed, with elections in three months, and all the local, national armies disbanded. They had far more thermonuclear warheads than they knew what to do with. And when they heard the word on what we collect in taxes, as opposed to what they'd been paying . . ." She let that trail off. The Concordat standard rate of seven percent, divided fairly between property and income taxes, had been the last, unanswerable argument for unification; the citizens of the world had been paying anywhere from twenty to seventy percent.

"For planetary council . . ." Steldan began to ask.

"Secretary Redmond and I followed your advice exactly," she reassured him. "Although we'd both privately come to the same conclusion. Take the people who were in power, presidents, kings, and all, and leave them in office. They make up the current council. Although we had to remove the patents of nobility from the kings." She frowned. "They hated that, I'm sure you can guess. But they had no right to any exalted status. What's that saying? 'No truce with kings?'"

Steldan nodded. "That's the way we've found best." Another thought took him. "What about Potok Empellimin?"

De la Noue gave him a sour grimace. "He's no longer our concern; he belongs to the doctors. And I don't think that even they can help him. He's as determined a man as I've ever seen, and as crazy. The doctors use various phrases; 'paranoia, schizophrenia, psychosis.' Simply put, though, he's out of the picture for the rest of his life." She sighed. "He actually seems to believe that the survivors of the Theury war are better off now than they were, because they're free of the taint of our technology. When he was told that we were helping to rebuild the continent, he flew into a frenzy. He is constantly railing against fusion reactors as the lowest form of evil worship—his words, not mine." She glanced at Steldan. "None of this news is to be released for a while, by the way. We're waiting for the right moment to let it out."

"Who is in control of Theury continent?"

"We are. Military authority. Commander Denis is temporarily in charge. Things are looking better there by the day. I have high hopes that the Theuran citizens will participate in the upcoming elections."

"Good luck, Admiral."

"Thank you, Commodore."

By view-screen, they watched the lowering of the old national flags, and the raising of the green-and-silver. The world had been saved . . . too late, and almost against its will. The experiment, which should never have been started, had been ended. For some, though, hope was refreshed.

Loyd Shayler forced himself to a stiff and correct politeness as he sat to evening dinner with his family and with the two former leaders of the bandits. They were good workers, he had to admit, and they caused no trouble. Without the Marine detachment present, though, he hated to imagine what disloyal commotion these disarmed brigands might make.

The thought of the Marine company brought a slight smile to Loyd's mind, if not to his face. So far, he'd snubbed their leaders in every way open to him. Here he was, in his own home, eating the day-meal with men who had been his enemies, while those outsiders, those star-tyrants had never been invited within. And that was the way it would stay.

After all, the bandits were local men and women, driven from their homes by the war. He himself could have been in their situation. But the off-worlders . . . Loyd clenched his fist below the thick table. The off-worlders were interfering, swaggering busybodies who had nothing better to do than get in the way. *Hell, they even stop me from disciplining my own workers, to say nothing of the bandits. I'll be damned glad when they finally leave.*

Willa brought in the roast then, and his grim thoughts evaporated in the determined feasting that followed. *These ex-bandits are going to be okay.*

By the time the beer flowed, a working partnership and a real friendship had been fairly forged.

Fulmer Garvey, upon his return, had taken the trouble to reestablish his position as working foreman of advance Camp Epsilon. Whether or not he would have succeeded eventually—and he knew he would have—was a question rendered moot by the arrival of a large transport shuttle on the fifteenth day after his return. The bill of lading had addressed the supplies to "Fulmer Garvey, foreman, Camp Epsilon."

That night he had been elected mayor, and Jacob McGinnis, the previous mayor, had stepped aside without argument. Soon, Garvey discovered that the paperwork and other minutiae of running an advance camp were more demanding, in their way, than bossing a work-crew.

Night was falling on the seventh day since the arrival of that shuttleful of matériel. Garvey stood up from behind his desk in the rapidly darkening office. Papers, figures, and forms danced for a moment in the dusk before his eyes. He swept them away with an effort, and wandered toward the door.

That load of supplies had been signed for by someone named Athalos Steldan, not James Tyler. Garvey wondered, as he often had since coming back to the camp, where Tyler might be. Had he been executed, as he had feared? Or was he, as Garvey more than half suspected, on the run somewhere? The image of Tyler as a hunted man was so apt that for a moment Garvey smiled.

That was a man who was hunted indeed; hunted by a part of himself. How can you outrun your own fears, your own hatreds? Tyler certainly didn't know how. One step behind him, breathing down his neck, looking through his eyes, was a shadow that he couldn't flee. I'd have liked to have helped him; maybe I did, a little. But nobody can ever free him from himself.

Outside his office, Garvey shut and locked the door by feel. Shuffling his way through the pitch-black anteroom, he emerged after a moment out into the cool evening, kept almost warm by the late spring fog. It was a high fog, he noted, and that cheered him. On this night, of all nights, a thick, obscuring fog would be anticlimactic.

Within minutes he came to the central square of the camp, where the citizenry had gathered quietly. A ludicrously oversized switch had been set up, with its handle painted a garish red. In the darkness, it was barely visible, and the red looked almost black.

"What do you say, Mr. Garvey?" asked someone.

That stopped him. He hadn't come prepared to make a speech. *Keep it short,* he warned himself.

" 'Out of the war that belonged to us, we carve our blooded beginning.' " *Who wrote that, anyway?*

Thanks, James.

He threw the switch. Without a sound, the still darkness was floodlit, with lamps on tall poles casting harsh shadows, and lamps in windows shedding warm light. The camp, which had slowly become a town, glittered, and the field of scintillant sparks was spread below them. A glad, rosy glow was thrown back from the overcast sky.

Thanks, James. And then his voice, too, was lost in the general jubilation.

Grand Admiral de la Noue sat staring at the blank surface of the conference table, a cup of cold coffee forgotten at her elbow. She once again ran over the long chain of effort that had brought the Black Book into existence. It had been founded long, long ago, by a Grand Admiral whose name she knew only from history texts. It had been around, hidden in total secrecy, for most of that time.

And she had ended it. It struck her as ironic that one of the most lasting contributions she could have made this early in her career as a member of the Praesidium was the dismantling of an almost venerable institution. But no matter when founded, it had been ill-founded. She knew that she had done right.

Commodore Steldan tells me that the Book's operational codes have been expunged from the overall computer complex. He was clearly the right man to oversee the job. Chief of Intelligence Records? Too bad there's another ahead of him to fill Higgins's vacancy. Of course, I could override that consideration . . . but it would be poorly taken. Steldan understands, of course. He wasn't expecting that appointment.

Can I trust him? That thought stopped her for a moment. Where had it come from? *Of course I can trust him,* she thought, as her brow furrowed. *What could he do with something as inherently dangerous as the Black Book?*

Disregarding the direct order of the Grand Admiral is an insanity that I could expect from James Tyler—she frowned to think of him dead, although she'd seen him only once, and briefly—*not from Athalos Steldan. He is responsible for my appointment to Grand Admiral; he wouldn't disobey me. If I can't trust him, then there's no one on my staff I can trust.*

The Black Book. Who has hands steady enough to hold life and death themselves? Certainly it's a tempting idea; that's the most evil thing about it. It tempts the owner to use it, to make the judgment, without any check on his authority, and without any appeal.

I couldn't have borne the responsibility, simply because there are people whom I'd like to see out of the way. There are even people I'd like to see dead. I'll be honest; I'd rather not have the Black Book, partly because it would tempt me.

Her mind slid easily over the thought of a real and dangerous enemy, who might pose a threat to the Concordat, and how convenient his assassination could be.

There was an even more convenient possibility: that the Black Book be held by someone subordinate to her, acting in her interest, without her knowledge or responsibility. Of this, she never thought at all, or if she did, she was not aware of it.

*   *   *

Late into the night, wearing into the small hours that presage dawn, Tyler stood stiffly in the basement firing range of the Navy military police depot, crashing rounds through pasteboard targets. Warm in his right hand, the savage backblow of the heavy automatic pistol jolted his arm and shoulder. The room came to reek of burnt white powder; near-invisible fumes stung his eyes. Instead of the well-worn, snub-nosed pistol he once used on business, he had selected a hellishly large automatic pistol, similar to the hunting pistol he had once carried. Small pieces flew from the battered target figure, draped as it was with the shredded remains of one of his old sweaters. He was alone.

In his pocket was a blank piece of paper, which, before the time-printed dyes in the ink had faded, had been a message from Steldan. It had informed him of the actions Steldan had taken. Now, by legal fiction, James Tyler the Navy Commander was dead, interred with honors on the homeworld. *Bury me where I lie fallen,* he quoted; *take my gun with you/ and slay my slayer.*

Legally dead, a gift from his once-target Steldan, yet he could still retain his name. The necessary computer-file alterations had been arranged quietly, efficiently—Steldan was nothing if not efficient—and Tyler remained at the Exonidas military base.

Getting shot had done something for him: It had made him more aware of what death really was. He strongly doubted that he would ever again be able to kill. But in truth, that disability had been coming over him slowly, perhaps for years.

He'd had Empellimin's corded neck huge in his gunsight and not fired.

Not long after he had left the hospital, his dreams had begun to turn ugly. Between timeless dream-imagery of carnage, of blood-showering slaughter, a different kind of image came to him. In a long line wandering through his mind, those that he'd killed filed past and faced him. There was no accusation from them; there was no need. He came to doubt his ability to face them.

The words of Steldan came back to him: "You've been the instrument of the death penalty too many times to be able to speak against it."

And before him, the words of Fulmer Garvey: "You're bent on suicide."

The rest of the night was an agony for him, as he emptied clip after clip into the target-mannikin that he so much wished was himself.

During that day, he slept, succumbing at last to the demands of his body. It was not restful, that sleep.

At three o'clock in the morning, after he had tossed fitfully for what seemed like twenty hours but was really ten, he threw himself into wakefulness, and groped in the dark room for a light switch.

It could no longer be borne.

He dressed, and descended the stairs of the apartment complex where he had his lair. Outside, on the street beneath the glaring street lights, waited a ground car. Steldan had seen to it that he was given the money that was his; the fellow had done that much. *But, legally at least, I'm a dead man, and I feel like one.* The car would enable him to get away for a few free hours.

The multi-lane wide roads left the city by several paths; Tyler chose the nearest. This one was nearly empty because of the hour. For long, meaningless miles it stretched, climbing always, gently, into the high mountains that surrounded the city of Exonidas. These mountains were, if Tyler remembered correctly, a subsidiary branch of the Nyecrags. In the darkness, there was very little to see beyond the patch of road illuminated by the headlights.

The wide-way branched; Tyler took the lesser road. Soon, he was following an ordinary two-lane highway. First on the right, then on the left, the roadway dropped off into deep chasms, bottomless, tempting. On the opposite side, the clay and cobblestone cliffs towered up out of sight. At the top of this first chain of high

hills, he found a small pass. Below it, the many lights
were visible in a small bastard community, nameless
in the enclosing darkness. The town, nestled comfortably in a small valley between drop-offs on two sides,
and impossible, climbing canyons and badlands on two
others, was turned, of necessity, inward in its view-
point. It presented no claims to the outside world, for
it felt no need of the outside world's approval.

For a cheerfully meaningless two hours he spoke
with the attendant at an all-night convenience store.
But ghosts from his past stalked him; he fled on, up
into the beckoning hills.

Onward, climbing, heading for the summit. Was he
advancing or retreating? The road became narrower,
less trustworthy. Tapering conifers replaced the gray-
shagged oaklike trees that had sparsely dotted the
high plains below. The horizon closed in; fog and great
looming trees reduced visibility to scant meters, and
made a tunnel of the road.

Fear. The road, the constricted view, the closeness,
the rush of the wind past the car, all conspired to lend
the motionless trip a nightmarish quality. Clinging to
rocky outcrops, the several small settlements that he
passed, each no more than four or five wooden buildings, all managed to look afraid. If they—secure behind low picket fences, beneath snow-patched roofs,
watched over by coldly alert security lights—could
look so terribly afraid, how was he to feel, hurtling
past on the endless road, bound from nowhere to nowhere, alone?

Soon it was light, although the thick fog made a
drifting twilight of the hour. He found a wide spot in
the road and parked. Cold wind blew the fog past his
face, and, after a few minutes of walking aimlessly, he
found himself on the lip of a precipice, looking straight
down a rocky cliff-face of some hundred and fifty meters. Between Tyler and the drop stood nothing more
than the rotted stumps of what once had been guard-
rail posts, planted there in years past when the road
was meant to be used. Closed now, the road-top cov-

ered with the detritus of years, the view was accessible only after the short climb on foot.

Straight down he could see a tumble of lifeless rocks, with here and there a dusty clump of undergrowth clinging to the steep surface. In clear weather, the view would open out into a wide vista of the descending hills flattening out into the eastern desert; that day, the patchy, drifting fog closed the view in, containing it.

He returned, fast, fleeing from himself, and came back to the city more confused than anything else.

The great roads led straight from the wilderness to the heart of the city; the vice district was directly ahead. He knew what he needed, what had prevented him from—he faced the truth—from leaping from that precipice, as part of him had wished to.

He remembered where he had first met Jill.

A sharp trepidation filled him. Mastering it, he parked the car beyond the fringe of the vice district and went ahead on foot. Soon Lady Titania's was before him.

"She can't see you now," warbled the headmistress.

Even as the black depression clamped down on his mind, he saw the hurt expression flash across the matron's face. What had she seen on his? Had he expressed rage? Or misery? Why, he asked himself, should he care what she thinks? What was he to either of them? "Can't see you now" is a brothel euphemism for "busy with another customer." That was all he felt himself to be to her: another damned customer.

He never afterward could clearly remember the next two hours. Since he was already in the worst part of town, he went looking for trouble. He didn't find it.

Damned fool I was to imagine I meant anything to her.

Before long it was noon. He'd been walking for several hours, without caring where his feet led him. With suddenly returning awareness, he looked up to find himself in a small, one-block park, carpeted with freshly mown grass, and with neat trails leading between the towering dry-branched trees and the thick, spiny hedges. Bordering one edge of the park, a tiny row of graves waited, with stones remembering heroes of forgotten wars, and their women and children. Away from these, he found a private spot and reclined gratefully.

Is there anywhere in a city of this size that a man can find privacy? An old woman, well-proportioned but gray, and frowning from her austere countenance, had long ago accustomed herself to using this spot at this time. Tyler became aware of her scrutiny—almost, she looked puzzled—but by turning away he tried to ignore her presence. He moved a little away, and stretched himself out to rest on the cool grass.

"You look miserable, child." The old woman was near him, speaking in a parched whisper. How could anyone move so silently? He recoiled. The quick motion startled her, and she scurried backward, catlike, and watched him warily from a slight distance.

Carefully, Tyler backed away, rising gently to his feet in such a way as to communicate harmlessness. He moved slowly, with the open ease needed when near children or frightened animals. He was preparing to leave, and had no wish to further alarm this old woman.

He didn't get far.

"Come back and sit down," she said imperiously.

He obeyed; for what reason, he could never have said.

She looked at him, meeting his gaze with great liquid eyes that seemed all pupil and no iris. Her face blurred in and out of distinction; her eyes grew huge.

"What's your name?" she asked. It almost seemed that she cared . . . cared greatly.

"James Tyler."

" 'James Tyler,' " she said, meditatively, pulling at the words and looking for a weak spot. A sharp glance. "I've said it once. When I've said it three times, James Tyler, will you trust me?"

"I . . . trust no one."

"Is there in truth no one that you trust, James Tyler?"

And because she seemed so earnest, he answered truthfully. "No one."

She nodded. "Give me your hand."

He complied. She glanced at him oddly. "Most people, when they are right-handed, give me their right hand."

Looking down, he saw his left hand cradled in her two, looking for all the world like something small and alive that she had caught and was holding. He began to withdraw it, and was stopped.

"Some strength," she said, "and some cleverness. Too much reserve. Fear. Tension. Hatred." Her eyes had drifted shut; she opened them. "You need me."

Over and over, in his mind, he leaped to his feet and ran; but his body sat motionless, inert, dead to his will. The urge to escape rose to a taut climax, and passed him, leaving him free of the trapped feeling he'd felt since he first saw her.

"Man of blood. You can never kill them all, for you are one of them."

"I know—" he snapped, and ground his teeth together to kill the rest of the sentence.

"And you can never kill yourself," she continued unperturbed, "for you are immortal. This is true, and you have always known it."

He had nothing to say.

"Now give me your hand."

He did.

Long minutes passed. Her eyes were closed, and even her breath seemed to be stilled. The sounds of the birds in the treetops came to him, and the birds' voices were making mock of him. "Fool that thou art; wretch, now black, and roasting fiercely. What of thee that burns now is no more than the light that glances off the tower, glinting now, but gone when night doth fall. What of thee that is true is within thee forever, and is of the strength of the tower forever. Be glad therefore; be among us in these treetops. A cat comes prowling, and perhaps you will not escape."

The woman's eyes opened, and she cocked her head to the side in a frighteningly birdlike fashion.

"What is her name?"

"Jill." He knew better than to lie to this woman.

"What is she?"

"She is a prostitute."

She slapped his hand, and he was very much surprised at how much it hurt. "No. She is not. Go to her, and see her with open eyes." The woman smiled, very briefly. "She loves you fully as much as you love her. She always has."

Tyler sat, unmoving, staring at this madwoman.

"Go!" she shrieked, and smote him heavily across the face.

He rose, flushing, and turned and ran from the park. He never again returned there, nor was able to retrace his steps, or find it on any map. He ran down the hill, between the houses, shops, trees, lots, and the filth that was this area's portion of humanity.

The streets flew past him, colorful, brash, vital. To every side of him, people stood, and sat, and were themselves. None lent him any particular interest.

As he neared the brothel, he pulled from his pocket his wallet, and emptied it of cash. At the brothel doorway he wheeled and entered, harsh of breath, his heartbeat singing in his ears. He threw the bundle of money—some nine hundred credits' worth—onto the table where the startled headmistress sat. Without pausing he hurled himself past her and into the rear of the building.

At Jill's door he paused . . . but only for an instant. The door flew wide to his first leg-jolting kick; he was inside instantly.

With strength he seldom needed to draw upon, he pulled the sweat-streaked man from atop her and set him roughly to the side. Wrapping her in her blanket, he took her in his arms and made the most spectacular departure of his career.

The scene will live forever in the lore of the city's vice district: The tall blond madman, with the strength of ten and an endless bankroll, tearing apart the brothel and leaving with the most beautiful of the women in his arms. He even had the story told to him, by people whose opinions he ordinarily would have respected. Apparently, he was never recognized.

Fifteen blocks away he stopped, satisfied himself that there was no pursuit, and gently deposited Jill beside him at a bus stop bench. She pulled her blanket more tightly about herself and eyed him critically.

"Do I get an explanation, James?"

He was breathing too heavily for a long speech, and could only nod.

"Fine. I'll wait." She composed herself with all the dignity that a beautiful woman can muster while waiting in public dressed only in a blanket. Tyler knew then what he should have known long ago: He loved her, never more than now.

"It's like this . . ." he began.

She cocked her head to the side in a disturbingly birdlike fashion, and with the impact that a bucket of ice water would have had upon him, the gesture dashed away his mirth. His voice and demeanor were serious as he spoke.

"I've decided that I love you, Jill."

"You have a strange way of showing it."

"Would you rather that I had waited?"

She grinned. "I don't care about *that*." Her grin faded. "Do you?"

"No, Jill, I don't. Let's get away from here."

"Is that a proposition?"

"No. It's a proposal."

She gazed long into his eyes. Not then, nor ever after, was he able to look away from her eyes.

"Let's go, then." She grinned afresh. "And all things considered, I'm glad you didn't wait." She wrapped her blanket about the two of them, and held him, whispering into his ear, "I love you, too. I always have."

"So I've been told."

BIO OF A SPACE TYRANT
Piers Anthony

"Brilliant...a thoroughly original thinker and storyteller with a unique ability to posit really *alien* alien life, humanize it, and make it come out alive on the page." *The Los Angeles Times*

A COLOSSAL NEW FIVE VOLUME SPACE THRILLER—
BIO OF A SPACE TYRANT
The Epic Adventures and Galactic Conquests of Hope Hubris

VOLUME I: REFUGEE   84194-0/$2.95 US /$3.50 Can
Hubris and his family embark upon an ill-fated voyage through space, searching for sanctuary, after pirates blast them from their home on Callisto.

VOLUME II: MERCENARY   87221-8/$2.95 US /$3.50 Can
Hubris joins the Navy of Jupiter and commands a squadron loyal to the death and sworn to war against the pirate warlords of the Jupiter Ecliptic.

VOLUME III: POLITICIAN   89685-0/$2.95 US /$3.50 Can
Fueled by his own fury, Hubris rose to triumph obliterating his enemies and blazing a path of glory across the face of Jupiter. Military legend...people's champion...promising political candidate...he now awoke to find himself the prisoner of a nightmare that knew no past.

Also by Piers Anthony:
The brilliant Cluster Series—
sexy, savage interplanetary adventures.

CLUSTER, CLUSTER I	01755-5/$2.95 US/$3.75 Can
CHAINING THE LADY, CLUSTER II	01779-2/$2.95 US/$3.75 Can
KIRLIAN QUEST, CLUSTER III	01778-4/$2.95 US/$3.75 Can
THOUSANDSTAR, CLUSTER IV	75556-4/$2.95 US/$3.75 Can
VISCOUS CIRCLE, CLUSTER V	79897-2/$2.95 US/$3.75 Can